VERTICAL WORLD ∀

THE SHROUD OF ÆTHERIA

BY BRIAN CRAWFORD

EPIC Escape

An Imprint of EPIC Press
abdopublishing.com

The Shroud of Ætheria

Vertical World: Book #1

abdopublishing.com

Published by EPIC Press, a division of ABDO, PO Box 398166, Minneapolis, Minnesota 55439. Copyright © 2019 by Abdo Consulting Group, Inc. International copyrights reserved in all countries. No part of this book may be reproduced in any form without written permission from the publisher. Escape™ is a trademark and logo of EPIC Press.

Printed in the United States of America, North Mankato, Minnesota.
052018
092018

♻

Cover design by Christina Doffing
Images for cover art obtained from iStockphoto.com
Edited by Gil Conrad

Library of Congress Cataloging-in-Publication Data

Library of Congress Control Number: 2018932901

Publisher's Cataloging in Publication Data

Names: Crawford, Brian, author.
Title: The shroud of Ætheria/ by Brian Crawford
Description: Minneapolis, MN : EPIC Press, 2019 | Series: Vertical world; #1
Summary: On his sixteenth birthday, the Ætherian Rex Himmel learns that he is special—but no one will tell him why. Ordered by Ætheria's leader to join the militaristic Ætherian Cover Force, Rex soon finds himself involved in an investigation of several mysterious, frozen Cthonian bodies that have been discovered in Ætheria. Just as his team finds a reason for the bodies' appearance, Ætheria's power plant is destroyed in a violent attack from below.
Identifiers: ISBN 9781680769111 (lib. bdg.) | ISBN 9781680769395 (ebook)
Subjects: LCSH: Great powers--Fiction. | Survival--Fiction--Fiction. | Revolutions--Fiction—Fiction. | Science fiction--Societies, etc--Fiction | Young adult fiction.
Classification: DDC [FIC]--dc23

T 27185

This series is dedicated to Debbie Pearson.
Thank you for everything.

PROLOGUE

SIX MILES ABOVE PLANET CTHONIA'S SURFACE, the seeds of war were sprouting.

For the eight hundred years of its existence, the stratospheric colony Ætheria had never seen anyone from below. Perched atop thousands of stratoneum struts reaching thirty thousand feet to the ground like stilts, the twenty-four man-made islands sheltered Ætheria's two thousand inhabitants from sub-zero temperatures, a howling jet stream, and ultraviolet rays from a merciless sun. Since they'd built the colony and left Cthonia centuries before, the Ætherians knew there was no reason to go back down. There was no food. The rain was acidic. And there was no air below the toxic, endless Welcans cloud of fermionic lithium separating the two worlds. Of course, there had always been rumors of a lost tribe of animal-like Cthonians who still roamed around in the wasteland below. But until that one night in April, the two worlds had remained apart.

Clinging to the southern edge of Island Two, Ætheria's Power Works purred over the wind. Unlike the Ætherians who depended on it for their survival, the teardrop-shaped structure never slept. Day and night, its Proboscis—a stratoneum tube twenty yards in diameter and six miles long—drew up water and cthoneum gas from the planet's surface. Once inside the building, the water was filtered and pumped to Ætheria's islands through a network of pipes, where it was used for drinking, cleaning, and watering crops in the colony's two biodomes. As for the explosive gas, this was used to power turbines, generating electricity and life-sustaining heat. Just above the Welcans cloud, the Proboscis also pulled in oxygen, but very few people in Ætheria knew what it was being used for . . .

Between ten and eleven o'clock that night, a new sound rose above the turbines' usual droning. Itself barely audible above the wind, a dull metallic grating rattled just underneath one of the three Proboscis access covers. An Ætherian Cover Force guard standing right next to the manhole-shaped hatch would not have even heard the scratching, clawing, and pushing that was loosening the cover from its frame. In the pale light of the stars and waning moon, the hatch was almost invisible—only a black circle in a dark gray field of artificial turf.

Little by little, the thick metal cover inched upward. Then, with a popping swoosh, a burst of pressurized air spurted from underneath as the hatch lifted and two sets of human fingers appeared around its perimeter.

"That's it!" a muffled voice hissed from below.

"Hurry up, I can't go much more," a woman's voice answered.

"Don't worry."

"Get it off!"

"Good God, it's cold."

"Uh, my head . . ."

With a sustained grunt, the person below lifted and slid the cover onto the turf. The hands reemerged from the darkness and planted themselves onto the sides of the hole. In one graceful movement, the person hauled himself out and stood, bracing himself against the wind.

Squinting against the freezing jet stream, the man looked around. A respirator mask hid his mouth and nose. He wore black pants, a black sweater, a loaded utility belt, and a shiny, black, oblong backpack that looked like a large football strapped to his back. His legs trembled from having spent the past day climbing six miles up the Proboscis with no time to rest apart from short breaks on service platforms inside the tube. As he steadied himself, his partner followed. The two gripped each other's shoulders with one hand each, holding each other up.

For the first time in eight hundred years, Cthonians had arrived in Ætheria.

When he'd caught his breath, the man stepped back to the hole and peered in.

"What's going on?" he shouted, cupping his hands around his mouth. "Get up here!"

"Go on, we're coming," came the answer from below.

"Are you okay?" the man asked.

"Something's wrong with Errie."

"What is it? Has he gotten worse?"

"Jackson, just go. We're coming, I said! But hurry . . . my head . . . the air . . . " The voice trailed off.

Jackson looked back up at his partner.

"Look, Mira. Máire said the entrance would be north. That way. We've gotta move fast. Let's split up. You go around the other side of the building. I'll do this one. Does your radio work up here?"

"Lemme check." Mira lifted a small receiver from

her belt and clicked TRANSMIT. "Jackson, testing. Hello?"

Jackson's radio clicked alive and Mira's crackly voice rose from his belt.

"Good," he said. "Let's move. Radio if you find anything."

"What if we see someone?"

"Just raise your hands and explain who we are. Ask for help. That's why we're here."

"Got it."

The two separated. Jackson turned toward the left-hand side of the building and walked with stiff legs. Mira went to the right.

As he moved, Jackson wiggled his toes inside his boots and flexed his hands again and again into tight fists. He'd been in the open air for less than a minute, but he already felt the cold biting at his feet and hands as his skin cells began to crystallize. Behind them, none of the other four Cthonians in their team emerged from the tube, even though they had a clear mission: contact the Ætherians immediately and get water.

Despite the cold, his fatigue, and his trepidation about making contact with the Ætherians, Jackson couldn't suppress a sense of wonder. Cthonians had always known about Ætheria, but until the Ætherian refugee Máire fled to Cthonia sixteen years earlier, all anyone had to go on was rumors . . . and those who'd been tossed from above. For one thing, Jackson had never seen stars or the moon before, only the churning yellowish cloud that permanently blocked out the sky. Now, their bluish light cast a dull pallor on the new world he was discovering. It was a world built on man-made islands floating above the clouds, though he knew they were held up by poles and thousands of wires, invisible in the moonlight. On the few islands he could see, bulbous buildings rose like giant bubbles. Some were circled by six-foot-wide passages running around the base like massive pipes coiling around a dome. Each island was several hundred yards long by two or three hundred yards wide, and they stood apart from each other by twenty or thirty yards. No barriers or protective walls lined the edges. One slip too close and a deadly, six-mile drop was what awaited. But how did the Ætherians move from island to island? In the low light, Jackson couldn't see.

"There!" he snapped to himself, yanked from his amazement by something moving up ahead. He halted and grabbed his transmitter.

"Mira, I see someone."

The radio crackled, and Mira's voice came through.

"Got it. Do you want me to come? There's no one over here, but I think I see a door."

"Hang on," Jackson said. "I'm going to initiate contact."

"Be careful."

Click. The radio fell silent.

Twenty yards in front of Jackson, a human form strode from around the building's corner and toward the Cthonian. The person walked slowly but deliberately, like one meant to be patrolling at night. In the low light, Jackson could make out no features, only a silhouette. But already he could see that, like the Ætherian Máire back on Cthonia, the person was at least a foot shorter than the average Cthonian. Were all Ætherians this small?

"Help!" Jackson shouted, speeding to a jog to greet the Ætherian. "Please! I've got people here who are dying, and . . ."

He didn't finish his sentence. At the sound of his voice, the Ætherian spun toward Jackson and blinded him with a searing white headlight that clicked on, piercing the darkness. The Ætherian didn't speak or make any noise, but in the next second Jackson fell to the ground, writhing in pain and screaming as one hundred thousand volts coursed through his body. From his back, his smooth pack rocketed off into the night, projected by a blast of compressed air that sent the pack over the edge and hurtling down below.

On the other side of the darkened building, Jackson's screams sent Mira running, searching for some place to hide.

"Bernuac HQ, this is Ama 6876," the Ætherian who'd fired spoke into her Tracker, a watch-like device on her wrist that all members of the Ætherian Cover Force wore to track their movements and monitor their conversations. She was dressed in a skintight, insulated suit that left only her mouth and nose uncovered. Even her eyes were hidden behind black goggles. She wore no mask, but huffed unobstructedly into the thin air. "Reporting the presence of what looks like a person from . . . below. A spy, maybe. I don't know. But definitely Cthonian." She stepped up to Jackson, who lay motionless on the artificial turf, his face partially blocked by his respirator mask.

There was a pause. From farther behind her, a second Ætherian ran up in similar dress, his pistol-shaped weapon drawn.

"What is it? What happened?" the second arrival panted, his headlamp casting a circle of white on the inert body. "Oh, my God . . . " He doubled over, trying to catch his breath. At this altitude, any effort beyond a slow walk always resulted in vertigo and lightheadedness. He should've known better not to run. In Ætheria, people had to move slowly. Otherwise they risked hypoxia—a dangerous lack of oxygen.

Before Ama could answer, a static-filled answer from Bernuac HQ spurted from her wrist.

"What's that? A spy? How do you know? How can you tell?"

"I'm not sure, but he's definitely Cthonian. He's tall and pale. I dazed him with my Stær gun. He's here but unconscious."

"A Cthonian? You can't be . . . but . . . how? Is anyone with you?"

"Yes, Challies is."

"Okay. Stay there. The Head Ductor will want to know this."

"The Head Ductor? At this hour?" Ama's already pounding heart beat even quicker at the mention of

Ætheria's leader. What would he do? How would he react? Usually he personally got involved only when someone was going to be Tossed—thrown from the edge of one of the islands as capital punishment for a serious misstep. And, as everyone knew, most missteps in Ætheria were serious.

"Yes, hang on." There was a click and Ama's Tracker went quiet.

"You dazed him?" Challies asked, inspecting the Cthonian.

Ama nodded, causing her headlamp light to waver.

"Yes. Just in case."

"In case what? Are there more?" Challies looked around, pointing his Stær gun into the dark. "How did he get here?"

"No idea, but . . . " she paused, looking up. "Why is he here?"

"Did he say anything to you?"

"He shouted and ran at me. I might've panicked,

but it had to have been an attack. Right?" Her hands trembled as she spoke.

"But what if he . . . " Challies began. Ama couldn't see it, but his face twisted as memories of a past trauma surfaced. "The Head Ductor will Toss him."

"How do you know that?"

"I've seen it before. I . . . " he hesitated, looking down at his Tracker. He knew that Bernuac HQ would hear—and report—anything he said. "I just know that . . . "

"Ama 6876?" the voice from Bernuac HQ spurted from her Tracker.

"Yes?"

"Stay there. The Head Ductor's on his way, along with more ACF. He wants Ætheria searched for any more Cthonians. Every inch. All the buildings. All the storage and larder spaces under the island surfaces. Everything. And now."

"What about the Cthonian?"

"He's going to take care of him himself."

ONE

The Next Morning

WHEN ÆTHERIAN REX HIMMEL AWOKE ON his sixteenth birthday, two ACF Protectors stood at the foot of his bed. The name patches on their ultralight, insulated AeroGel suits read CHALLIES 2496 and ROMAN 3366. Each carried a holstered Stær gun at his waist, and each wore the official uniform of the Ætherian Cover Force: a dark blue AG suit, a rank badge in the center of his chest, and a Tracker on his wrist. Their darkened UV goggles dangled around their necks, leaving circular red marks around their eyes. No need to wear them inside. In addition to his uniform, Roman wore a small oxygen canister on his back, a small plastic tube winding under his nose and connecting to the tank. The tank hissed and clicked as he breathed. Roman was also in the Ætherian High Command. And this role meant he was afforded the luxury of supplemental oxygen.

"Rex," Challies said calmly, just as the boy began to stir. Hearing the strange voice made Rex sit up and gape at the two Protectors, his right eye and the right side of his mouth visibly drooping, paralyzed by an accident at birth. Because his house was heated, he was dressed only in his underwear and a T-shirt. As did all Ætherians, he wore his light-blue AG suit and UV goggles only to go outside.

"What?! Who are you? What are you doing? Dad . . . ?" Rex blurted, his misshapen mouth slurring his words. With startled eyes, Rex looked beyond the two Protectors through his bedroom door, hoping to hear or see his foster dad. As he called out, he doubted he would be there. As head of Ætherian Energy and Survival, Franklin Strapp was almost always gone, working on the adjacent island of Tátea, in Ætheria's Power Works. Even though Rex had lived with Franklin for his entire sixteen years, he often felt more like an orphan. His mom had disappeared when he was a baby, and all his foster dad really did was make sure Rex was fed and clothed, and that he stayed out of the way.

"Franklin's at work," Roman said.

Of course, Rex thought.

"How did you get in? What's going on?" Rex eyed the two men warily. He knew the Ætherian Cover Force was meant to protect Ætherians, though from what, he could never figure out. As far as he could tell, the only real dangers in the stratospheric colony came from the environment: cold, ultraviolet radiation, and wind. Whenever he brought the ACF up to his foster dad, Franklin only became evasive, quickly changing the subject and mumbling contradictory things about "no missteps in Ætheria" and "all bark and no bite," as if he were hiding something from Rex but really wanted to tell him the truth.

"How we got in is not really the point, is it?" Roman answered, casting a side glance at Challies. "But you need to get up. We have to go."

Sitting up fully but holding his covers around his waist, Rex wiped the sleep from his eyes.

"Go? I've got school. What do you mean? Go where?" Rex's eyes fell on Roman's oxygen tube— it was the same kind his foster dad wore every day. Seeing this triggered a pang of irritation. How many times had Rex argued with Franklin about these oxygen tanks? How many times had he asked for one? And how many times had Franklin explained to him that only members of the Ætherian High Command were allowed to have them? And how many times had Rex complained that others in Ætheria needed them?

Challies took a deep breath.

"We can't tell you everything. Suffice it to say that you are required to report to Bernuac HQ by 0800 today for conscription and deployment."

Bernuac HQ? Rex had heard his foster dad mention the ACF headquarters a few times in the past, but Rex had never set foot there. Located toward the northern end of Ætheria, it was a massive building with a high roof and no windows. "So people can't see in," Franklin had said. "For training and organization . . . that kind of thing." Because he didn't have clearance, all Rex could do was look at it from neighboring islands and wonder.

"Deployment? Conscription?" Rex asked. "What do you mean? For what? Have you talked to my dad?"

"We haven't, no," Roman said, his voice clearer and purer than Challies's. "But he knows. This decision has come from the Head Ductor himself. You have no choice. Neither do we. He has taken a keen interest in you, and he has made a decision about your future. He wants you in the ACF."

Hearing Ætheria's leader mentioned, Rex stood up and faced the two in his underwear and T-shirt. A tingling of apprehension filled his chest.

"The Head Ductor?" Rex felt his voice begin to tremble, but he tried to hold his chest out and show confidence. No one dealt with the Head Ductor. Rex had heard the rumors . . . not from Franklin, but from others. Behind closed doors, everyone whispered that the HD got involved in Ætheria's affairs only when there was to be a Tossing. Everyone murmured that the HD was not to be toyed with, and that there were no missteps in Ætheria. Everyone suspected it was really the Ætherian Council and the ACF that administered the colony, but rumors often changed, and they were never good.

"As of today, you are an ACF recruit," Roman said.

"What? ACF? I'm sixteen! I've got two years to go, and even then it's not required. Why . . . ?"

Roman held up his hand to silence Rex. As Roman spoke, Challies kept his eyes on Rex. His features seemed soft, kind even, whereas Roman seemed tense, ready to pounce.

"We know the rules. An exception is being made. You will find out more about your assignment, duties, and service once you arrive at Bernuac HQ."

Rex looked back and forth between the two. His thoughts raced. Because his foster dad was part of the Ætherian High Command, Rex had never paid much attention to the ACF—in his mind, they'd always been little more than kids playing dress-up with toy guns, even though his dad would mumble about "no missteps." In many ways, Rex's position as the son—albeit foster son—of one of the most powerful men in Ætheria had led him to develop a subconscious feeling of privilege, that he was almost untouchable, even. And this feeling had gotten him in trouble on more than one occasion: In school, he'd been suspended once for arguing with a teacher. And with his friends, he always accepted dares, even if that meant taking risks. Added to this was his insecurity about his facial deformity, as well as having a broken family. He never wanted people to think he was weak. He never wanted people to doubt his abilities. He never wanted people to whisper about him behind his back. And he never wanted them to suspect the true pain that he held in his heart . . .

"I don't . . ." he began, trying to articulate his words as clearly as possible. "Wait. No. I need time. I need to talk to Dad. I need . . ."

"No," Roman interrupted. "There is no time. The order has been given. And, as you will see, you are needed because a mission is under way. Something has happened here in Ætheria. Last night. And you will have a part to play. The other ACF are getting ready. You will join them. Now."

Rex felt impatience struggling with fear of the Head Ductor. Why would he suddenly be interested in Rex? Rex had never even seen the HD. Could this be something his dad had arranged? After all, his dad knew the HD and even conferred with him about his work. But wouldn't Franklin have said something to Rex? Warned him? Given him a choice?

"Something's got to be wrong," Rex said, trying to speak with a determined voice. "You can't just come in like this without my dad—my guardian—around. You said it yourself: there are rules."

Roman and Challies stood stoically, as if giving

Rex space to vent. His breath began to hiss as he tried to inhale enough air to keep from getting dizzy. He paused, panting. When he had caught his breath, he turned up his palms and shrugged his shoulders as if to say, "Now what?"

"Get dressed." Roman spoke with a friendly voice, but his tone was clearly more of a demand than a request. "We don't have much time."

Challies looked at Roman and back at Rex.

"No, I want to talk to my dad first. Can't I at least do that? Or at least can't I talk to someone else on the Council?"

"I'm going to ask you one time and one time only. I am delivering to you a direct order from the Head Ductor. Are you saying yes, or are you saying no? Think carefully about your answer."

"What? No, I mean, yes, just, yes. Wait. Just wait." Rex's voice quivered. "Let me at least message my dad before I do anything." Looking away from the Protectors, Rex attempted to push by them and leave the room. Roman grabbed his arm and squeezed, but Rex broke free and slid to Roman's left. Challies stepped in and grabbed Rex with both hands, while Roman thrust Rex back, his lips tightened and his face flushed. He pulled his left hand close to his mouth and spoke into his Tracker.

"Bernuac HQ, this is Roman 3366. The boy has not given a yes. He has attempted to flee."

"What? Flee?! Wait!" Rex snapped, panic swelling. "All I did was ask to talk to my dad first! I'm not doing anything wrong! I wasn't running away—I was getting my NotaScript!"

Roman ignored him, while Challies shifted in place, clearly uncomfortable. A reply crackled through Roman's Tracker.

"Roman 3366, you have permission to daze. Level Two only. Take care. He's important. You must bring him."

"Yes, thank you."

Roman looked back at Rex. He lowered his left hand, put his right on his Stær gun, and quickly flipped a knob with his thumb. A high-pitched whine filled the room.

"You will talk to your dad," Roman said, his voice bizarrely reassuring. "I'm sorry for this, but you must report to Bernuac HQ, and now. No missteps. Never forget."

With that, he drew his Stær gun and fired at Rex, who fell backwards onto his bed.

TWO

WHEN REX CAME TO, HE WAS LYING IN A PER-
fectly cylindrical, five-yard-wide pink room
with rounded walls, a circular ceiling, and a circular
floor, like a cross-section of a massive tube. In front
of him, a smooth, polished round wall smirked back,
and above, the ceiling glowed purple. He was now
fully dressed—not in his AG suit, but in loose-fitting,
soft clothes. He had no memory of dressing himself, nor could he remember how he'd gotten there.
Where was he?

Rex sat up. But as soon as he moved, his jaw
screeched with an inaudible yet skull-throbbing

frequency—one that threatened to loosen his teeth and rupture his eyeballs. The sound was like ten dentist drills boring into his molars at the same time. Rex couldn't hear the sound. He couldn't see any speakers. It was more as if it were pulsing out of his skeleton and through every inch of his body.

Rex wasn't chained or shackled, but he couldn't move.

Head motionless, he closed his eyes against the pain. He froze. The sound stopped.

When the door clanked and swooshed open, Rex jumped. The Pulse again coursed through him, causing him to groan. He tried not to move anything else—his jaw, his hands, his shoulders. It's not that the sound waves were painful, but he'd never wanted to die more than during those brief moments when they threatened to unravel every nerve in his body.

"Rex Himmel?" a familiar voice behind him broke the silence. Because of the round walls, his question boomed much louder than if they had been out-side—every note seemingly directed straight at Rex's throbbing ears. The man snapped his fingers. The snap thundered into the distance.

"I am Protector Challies of the ACF. This is Protector Roman. We met this morning." Challies's footsteps clumped around Rex from the right. Challies entered his field of vision and Roman stepped in from the left. Seeing the two men, Rex remembered the events from the morning: their sudden appearance in his bedroom, their orders, the HD being mentioned, and then the dazing . . . But why? And what time was it?

Over their AG suits, both wore the dark blue uniforms of Ætheria's Cover Force, which vibrated against the pink background of the room. They had donned shiny, black leather boots; a utility belt holding weapons, one of which Roman had used on Rex; folded manacles; a sheathed utility knife; a glistening badge affixed to the center of their stomachs; and a cap-and-mask combination that, on Roman, was attached to a backpack supply of oxygen. Roman still wore the plastic air supply tube that snaked from his nose to the tank on his back.

"You can talk," Challies continued, his voice soft, "I've ordered the Pulse lowered for small movements—your jaw, your head—enough for you to talk, to answer . . . You know what will happen if anything else moves. For the record: can you confirm that you are Rex Himmel?"

Rex nodded and studied the two without seeming to stare. He kept his head facing forward. Unlike that morning, Roman seemed to be there for backup. He didn't say anything, and his hands were empty. While Challies spoke, Roman circled Rex like a moon in orbit. His eyes left Rex's only when he passed behind him. Challies, however, circled in the opposite direction, his eyes shifting from an open metal binder in his left hand to Rex's face, as if trying to read a clue—something that might help what felt like an interrogation. As they spoke, the two never stopped moving.

"Yes. That's me."

"Do you know why you are here?"

"Where's 'here'?"

"Tátea. Interrogation and detention facility."

"I thought Tátea was just where the Power Works was?" Rex scanned his memory for any signs that anything other than power generation occurred on this island. But he found nothing—nothing his foster dad may have said and no clues from just looking at Tátea's buildings from adjacent islands.

Challies shot a glance to Roman. Challies shook his head.

"No. No one aside from the Ætherian High Command knows what this annex does. But don't worry about that. You need to answer our question. Do you know why you are here?"

"No, of course not," Rex snapped. "Why would I? You barged in this morning, and now I'm here. Does my dad know this? Do you know who he is?"

"Hmm," Challies either laughed or stifled a belch—Rex couldn't tell. "You are here," he said in a raspy voice, "because you resisted a direct order from the Head Ductor. And you tried to flee. We both saw you."

Rex started to protest, but Challies held up a hand.

"You were summoned by the HD himself to Bernuac HQ for ACF conscription. You said no. We heard you. That is the definition of resistance. You should know that working against the HD will land you in more trouble than you can imagine. No one wants that. Right?"

"But I didn't say no, I just . . . " Rex hesitated.

"You should've just come. And yes, we do know who your dad is. Franklin Strapp, head of Ætherian Energy and Survival. But in this case, it doesn't matter. We've got a job to do. And you need to decide—here, now—if you want to resist or accept and join up, sixteen or not. It's not a death sentence, you know. Do you really want to make a big deal of this? We're talking about conscription. It's not permanent; you should know that. But resisting the Head Ductor can lead to a permanent end."

Challies and Roman looked Rex straight in the eyes. Challies seemed to be mulling something over, but Roman's expression was empty. Challies's eyes went blank. He seemed lost in a dream. Rex thought he saw a flash of anger appear in the Protector's face, but it disappeared as quickly as it had appeared.

The hatch clicked behind Rex. His ears popped as the room's pressure shifted. The door opened, and someone stepped in.

"Rex, do you know what they do to people who resist?" the new voice said.

Great, Rex thought. His face burned. He tightened his lips and turned to face his foster dad. When he wasn't ignoring Rex, all he seemed to do was argue with his foster son. Why can't you stop getting into trouble at school? Why can't you keep your stuff in order? Why can't you make up your mind about what you want to do after school? You're sixteen—it's time! Rex was already fed up with his dad's bickering, and he wasn't thrilled to add this blown-up run-in with the ACF to the mix.

Franklin Strapp stepped in front of his foster son and positioned himself between Challies and Roman. Rex expected Franklin to be furious—red in the face and veins bulging—but he was calm. No, disappointed. He looked as if Rex had just smashed his dreams in one kick. The muscles in his face were relaxed and his shoulders drooped. He was still wearing his AG suit. He didn't even put on his uniform to come in. He had pulled his goggles over his head, leaving deep red rings around his slanted eyes. Despite his dark skin, his eyes twinkled with despair. Like Roman, he wore an oxygen canister and supply tube. As he spoke, the canister hissed and clicked with each inhale.

"Can we have a few minutes?" Franklin said to Challies. The Protector looked at Franklin and tightened his jaw. He glanced at Roman. Challies skimmed over something written at the top of his metal clipboard. He puffed air through his nose and nodded to Roman.

"Five minutes," Challies said. "And then we need his answer. The Head Ductor needs his answer."

Challies shot Rex an imploring look and clumped towards the hatch.

"Can you turn off the Pulse?" Franklin asked. "All the way?" He was looking over Rex's shoulder at the two Protectors. Without answering, they shuffled from the room. Their footsteps disappeared behind the metallic click of the closing hatch. Two seconds later, three high-pitched beeps chirped from above the ceiling.

"You can move," Franklin said.

Rex relaxed his shoulders and turned around. He rubbed his eyes and looked for the door. The walls were smooth. If his back hadn't been turned to the hatch, he would've thought the room was seamless.

Rex looked at his foster dad, whose eyes were on him. Franklin held Rex's lopsided gaze for a few seconds then inched to the room's edge, lost in thought. He ran his right hand across the circular wall as he spoke.

"Look," he began, keeping his eyes on the wall as he moved. He entered into a slow but wide orbit, much like Challies and Roman. Maybe that's why this room was round. Maybe when the questioners circled, the person in the middle would become more and more disoriented. But Rex didn't feel confused or disoriented, just irritated and anxious.

"It's been a tough year for us," Franklin said. "But I'm not going to let this get me worked up. Yes, you received an order from the Head Ductor. Not saying yes immediately can land you in a lot of trouble."

"But, Dad, what about the . . . "

"Stop," Franklin held up his hand and lowered his eyelids. "I know what you're going to say: The ACF. You don't like them. You think they're a waste of time and just puppets, or whatever it was you've always said. I get it. But right now, all that really matters is that if you don't agree to join the ACF, you face a trial. A trial! There are no missteps here, especially not when it comes to the HD. Haven't you heard anything I've ever said! Don't you know? And by the way, it makes no difference that you're sixteen. They find you guilty, and that's it." Franklin leaned into Rex's face, simultaneously covering his Tracker with his free hand. He whispered, "And it doesn't matter who I am or . . . " his voice trailed off, and he averted his eyes. Rex had the impression his foster dad had spoken to him more just now than in the past year. Rex had never heard him speak so much. So something must've been wrong, different.

"Or what?" Rex asked.

"Or who your mother was."

"Mom?" Rex's cheeks flushed. "What do you mean? Why did you say, 'was'? Is she dead? Alive? What do you know?"

Franklin shook his head and stepped away. "We've been through this." He brought his hand up to his mouth, regretting having spoken. "Look," he said, turning around. "I don't want you in trouble. And forget . . . "

"Forget what? My mother?" Rex's voice was incredulous. As Franklin spoke, Rex's thoughts flew to his many attempts—especially since he'd become a teenager—to find out something about his birth mom: who she was, where she was, if she was alive, and how he'd come to live with Franklin, a foster parent. Each time he'd brought it up, Franklin had always found some way to avoid the conversation. Rex had never mentioned her even to his friends, but she was never far from his mind.

"Yes. Forget about it. I can't have you get . . . tossed for this."

"Tossed?" Rex's limbs ran cold. "But . . . you . . . you always said the Ætherian Council was 'all bark and no bite.' Those were your words." Rex pointed at Franklin's chest to make his point.

Franklin furrowed his brow.

"Yes, I know, I know what I said," he snapped. "I also said there were no missteps. Just . . . look. Listen. Forget about all that. There's stuff . . . things . . . things go on that you don't know about. That I've never told you about, and that I can't. There's a lot that goes into running this place—more than you can imagine.

"When I found out what you did this morning, I spoke to the Head Ductor right away. Yes, him. And right now, you have a choice. Face trial and accept whatever happens . . . or you join the ACF. Your education can continue as an Auscultor with them."

"What? An Auscultor? What's that? And why me? Does no one else think this is strange? Are there going to be other sixteen-year-old recruits?" Rex's voice grew louder as he spoke.

At Rex's question, Franklin's face flushed, and he moved closer to his foster son. "Will you be quiet, before you end up getting yourself killed?" He glanced down at his Tracker, knowing that his words were likely being monitored. "You'll find out what's happening in time. Once you join, that is."

Rex fell silent. His thoughts churned. The ACF? Auscultor? He'd had plans with his life, and they hadn't involved the ACF. Up until just a few minutes ago, he'd even suspected this whole thing with Challies, Roman, and the HD was just a joke.

Still, there was something about his dad's behavior and what he said that planted a new seed in his mind: the seed of fear. His dad was talking more to him than he ever had, yet he was hiding something from him. But what?

Rex slid to a sitting position. Franklin stopped in front of him and looked down. Rex didn't look up. He buried his head in his hands. Sweat covered his forehead and temples. He sensed something was wrong. And that his foster dad needed an answer. Now.

Franklin tapped Rex's foot with his thermal boot. Rex looked up. Against the purple glow of the ceiling, Franklin loomed over his foster son like a giant black silhouette.

"Now, Rex. The moment to decide is now! And you should know: if it weren't for my job, you'd already be on trial for resistance—period. Especially you." He paused. "You are different." He pulled his

NotaScript from his pocket, glanced at the glowing screen, and pocketed it. Rex tried to see what his dad had read on the handheld device. But Franklin had turned it off before he could get a glimpse.

"They'll be back, and they'll want an answer."

Rex stood up.

"Dad . . . what is happening? Why is everyone getting so worked up?"

"They just are," he shot back, leaning in so close Rex could feel the heat from his breath. "They're getting worked up because," he sighed, "there are no missteps in Ætheria. None."

From the other side of the door, footsteps approached.

THREE

THE HATCH OPENED, AND REX'S EARS POPPED. A rush of frigid air blew in and tousled his loose-fitting suit. Challies and Roman were back.

They stepped in, and the hatch slid closed behind them. Roman's eyes were as blank as before. Challies looked at Franklin. For a second, the two seemed to be communicating without speaking. Challies blinked and turned to Rex.

Despite the pink and purple glow of the room, Rex saw his father's face burn crimson. He tightened his lips and looked back to the Protectors.

"Let's show him the bodies," Franklin said. He

looked at Rex. "This should help you make up your mind."

Bodies? A hint of panic welled up in Rex's chest. What is he talking about?

Rex turned back around just in time to see Challies and Roman reaching forward to grab his forearms. They squeezed so tightly, he could feel his muscles squirming underneath their grip to get out of the way. His tendons seemed to pop. Rex groaned and pulled back, but the two Protectors were stronger. Challies reached to his belt and wriggled out a folded black cloth. He flapped it at his side, opening it up. It was a hood.

"He won't need that," Franklin said. Challies jerked his head up at him and nodded. He looked over at Roman and tucked the hood back into his belt.

"Just as well," Challies said.

Roman shot his partner a look.

The hatch opened with a pop and a swoosh—a

thick, metallic door pulling to the side and disappearing into the wall.

"Where are we going?" Rex asked.

Franklin answered from behind.

"The morgue."

The four walked for about ten minutes—enough time for violent shivering to grip Rex with the threat of hypothermia in the unheated transit tubes between the buildings on Tátea. *So there's a morgue here, too?* Rex thought. *What else is hidden on this island?* The ACF Protectors had removed his AG suit, after all. And everyone in Ætheria knew that without your ultralight, insulated suit, the cold would kill you within an hour.

Rex walked down the tube with Challies and Roman at either side, each gripping his arm. Franklin walked behind them to the right. No one spoke.

The four walked along in a ribbed, translucent transit tube ten feet wide and barely six feet tall, which left them a good foot of headroom. Even though Rex had plenty of room, his breath came in quick, short bursts as claustrophobia crept in—a fear that had gripped him since childhood. When he was younger, doctors had suspected the phobia had originated during birth. Then, Rex had almost been strangled by his umbilical cord that had wrapped around his neck and held him trapped in the birth canal. He'd survived, but the incident had permanently left the right side of his face paralyzed, affecting his speech and vision in his right eye. Few places in Ætheria were so closed in as the transit tubes.

Every now and then, others passed them—from both directions. Those walking in the same direction always seemed in a hurry. Those coming in the opposite direction avoided looking at them, but ended up staring at Rex, as if he were some disfigured criminal. When others reached the four of them, they would squeeze against the side of the tube to pass, trying to put as much space between themselves and Rex as possible. Seeing their reactions, Rex felt his claustrophobia turning into anger. Why did they have to go out of their way to show their disgust? Couldn't they see he was a teenager? That he was with three employees of Ætheria?

Then it dawned on him: he was wearing what must've been a prisoner's uniform, he was unbound, he was not blindfolded, and he wasn't wearing an AG suit. At this altitude, leaving home without this ultra-light, protective suit was unthinkable.

The tubes twisted up, down, around, and through other tubes. No one talked.

After a few more minutes, the ACF Protectors stopped, and Rex's thoughts came back to the present.

They had arrived at an oval-shaped, purple door marked only with a pixelated code. Rex couldn't tell exactly where on Tátea they were, but he had the sense they were on the northern side of the island—the side directly opposite the massive Power Works. Franklin pushed his way around Roman and held his Nanokepp Card to the code. With a *beepbeep* and a click, the door slid open when it recognized

Franklin's unique, magnetized pass. He stepped aside to let the others through. He glanced at Rex and waved him in. Card still in hand, he fell in behind the other three. The four stepped in, and the door closed behind them.

Challies, Roman, Franklin, and Rex stood in a small room not much bigger than Rex's school classroom, but at least forty or fifty degrees warmer than outside. The sensation immediately began returning to Rex's hands and feet, but his stomach turned at the smell—a mixture of chemicals and refrigerated meat. He covered his nose with his hands, trying to focus on the smell of his sweaty palms instead of the reek. No one else in the room seemed to notice anything unusual.

The morgue was narrower than a classroom, with shiny stratoneum walls peppered with hundreds of little doors in neat rows, stretching from the floor to the ten-foot-tall ceiling. A small ladder was propped against the right-hand wall, its wheeled top affixed to a metal railing circling the room. The ladder's bottom ended in two similar wheels, which could let some-one roll anywhere around the room's perimeter. The doors themselves looked like small refrigerator doors, but ones whose handles closed over the outside of the door like a powerful latch. Rex wondered how many bodies lay behind the doors.

A gaunt watchman sat hunched over a metal desk just inside the entrance. He was typing some-thing into a NotaScript but paused and looked up. Franklin held out his card, and the man slid it under a flickering red scanner attached to the desk. Beep. The man read Franklin's credentials on the screen, and his faced blanched. He snapped from bored and bothered to submissive and jittery.

"Yes, sir?"

"We need to see number eight-seven-three."

"Council business?" The man stood and ran his palms over his AG suit.

"What else?"

The watchman shook his head as if realizing his mistake.

"Yes. Of course." He leaned over and opened his desk drawer, pulling out a set of thick gloves like oven mitts. "This way."

"We need to see all four."

The watchman stopped and turned on his heels.

"The frozen ones from this morning?" he asked.

"Yes."

The watchman nodded and turned. The others followed in silence.

"Over here." The watchman walked down the left side of the room to a door three rows up from the bottom and two columns from the room's corner. Just before stopping, he slid one of the gloves onto his left hand. Rex wondered if the man had memorized where everything was, because there were no markings on the doors. They stopped. The watchman placed his flattened palm on the door.

At his touch, the door hissed and sighed. With a click, it drifted open, releasing a thick cloud that seeped out and drifted to the floor, forming a thin layer of fog a foot deep. Once the mist thinned, Rex could see nothing but black on the inside of the door—no hints as to what the compartment contained. Only that whatever it was, it was being held in deep freeze.

In one fluid movement, the watchman pulled the door open with his right hand while reaching in with his left and grabbing a two-and-a-half-foot-wide silver tray. He pulled hard, straining under the effort. The tray emerged with a sound of metal scraping metal. The watchman pulled for another few feet and stopped, leaving the tray suspended in front of them at waist height. For the first time since leaving the interrogation room, Challies and Roman released Rex's arms and stepped back.

"Take a good look," Franklin said. "Tell me what you see."

Rex inched forward.

On the metal slab in front of him, a boy's body lay twisted and frozen, every inch glistening in a millimeter-thin, crystalline layer of hoarfrost. The boy seemed to be in his late teens. Rex gasped at the boy's physique, which was unlike anything he had ever seen.

First off, the boy was huge—at least six feet tall, a good foot taller than Rex or any of the boys he had grown up beside on Ætheria. He wore black pants and a dark blue, long-sleeved shirt. Rex couldn't tell what material the clothes were made of, but it was definitely something other an AeroGel suit. It looked light and ill equipped to keep in body warmth. *Had this been how he'd died? Of cold?* Rex wondered. He knew that if he wore that kind of clothing, he'd be dead within an hour. Ætheria was too cold for anything other than an AG suit.

The boy was also wearing some kind of utility belt not unlike the one worn by ACF Protectors—only his was bare, as if someone had taken everything that had been clipped to it. Open and empty fasteners circled his waist, their metallic clippers reaching up like small claws grasping out.

Underneath his clothes, the boy was muscular. His legs, torso, and arms held much more mass than

Rex's. In fact, his body mass was much greater than anyone's Rex had ever seen in Ætheria. It looked almost as if the boy had made a habit of exercising and taking some kind of drugs to become abnormally large. Rex's entire torso could fit inside the boy's chest cavity, with room to spare. His head seemed proportionally bigger than Rex's, too, as if his brain were one-and-a-half times larger.

Other than that, the boy's facial features seemed normal: eyes, nose, mouth, ears . . . Rex couldn't tell if it was the postmortem freezing or the boy's natural pigmentation, but his skin was sickeningly pale and his face spotted with darker flecks, like some sort of deformity that made Rex think of his own facial paralysis. Aside from his head and neck, the only other part of the boy's body that was exposed were his hands and left arm. Perhaps from whatever accident led to his death, his right leg lay bent mid-thigh at an awkward angle, and his sleeve had been ripped up to the shoulder. There, a bizarre but simple mark was etched onto his bulging deltoid:

▽

Despite his human features, the boy looked like a tattooed freak.

"They had to break his leg to get him loose," Franklin said, breaking the room's silence. "He was already almost completely frozen. They found him this morning at about five. While you were asleep. He had a mask on, but they took it off."

Rex looked into the boy's eyes. The irises were deep blue, but the pupils were clouded over.

"What do you make of that?" Franklin said.

"What?" Rex asked, looking up and removing his hands from covering his nose. He tried to breathe through his mouth to avoid the smell.

"This body. Does anything seem bizarre about it?"

Rex nodded. "Everything. Who is he? You said 'found'? Who found him? Where? What is this all about?"

Franklin didn't answer. Instead he turned to the watchman and nodded.

"Why don't you look at this and then tell me."

Before Franklin had finished his sentence, the watchman had opened three more doors, pulling out the metal trays. He slid three more bodies out, all of which hovered at waist height.

Rex scanned the bodies. Combined with the smell of the room and the spectacle of three dead people in front of him, Rex's head spun, and he felt sick. He looked to the ceiling and breathed deeply, trying to focus on one of the many white lights glaring down. Franklin stepped up and placed his hand on Rex's shoulder.

"What do you think is going on here?" he asked.

Rex scanned the bodies and shook his head.

The bodies were identical—older teenagers, tall, swollen heads, massive musculature, pale skin, cloudy eyes, inadequate clothing. Rex was just as at a loss for answers as his foster dad.

"Look," Franklin said, stepping up to one of the bodies and pulling a collapsible metal pointer from his pocket. The watchman stepped forward as if to protest, but checked himself and folded his hands behind his back.

Using the end of the pointer, Franklin pried the boy's left sleeve away from his forearm and worked it up. As the cloth wrinkled, the frost encasing it crackled and cristled. Franklin pushed harder, forcing the sleeve up and over the boy's shoulder. There, the same inverted triangle was etched into his skin.

"They all have this mark," Dad said. "Why?"

"Where did they come from?" Rex asked.

"We think they came up last night, we think—six total. And they all had masks."

"Six? Came up? From where? Where are the other two?"

"In custody. They were found roaming about on Tátea and are being tried right now, by the Head Ductor himself. Trials usually take a day or two. This will end in a Tossing, I'm sure."

"Where did they come from?" Rex repeated his question, his head spinning. What was going on?

Franklin stepped up and whispered into his foster son's ear.

"I'll tell you, but the ACF needs an answer. Are you with us? We need an answer right now! And I cannot protect you. You're being pulled into something because of . . . "

"What?"

"It's because of who you are."

"What do you mean, who I am?" Rex's thoughts churned around anything he could think of that made him different from others. Of all the Tossings he'd ever heard of, none had ever been because of just saying no or questioning some order from the HD. They'd been for much worse transgressions, such as stealing, hoarding water, or avoiding work. Rex's mom was gone, and he had been raised by one of the most powerful men in Ætheria. Was that it? It had to be. Other than getting into trouble every now and then at school, there was nothing else unusual about Rex. Nothing other than his drooping eye and misshapen face . . . But surely that couldn't be it?

Rex glanced once more at the bodies, but deliberately blurred his vision to avoid seeing their grisly details. As he gazed on them, his foster dad leaned in close and whispered in his ear.

"Powerful people are watching you, and have been watching you since you were born." His tone softened. "Don't look at this as a punishment. See it as an opportunity. You've been chosen, Rex."

Rex looked back at his foster dad. Thoughts swirled in his head. He knew he was getting different treatment because of who his foster dad was, but who were these "powerful people" who were watching him? Why? He couldn't shake the feeling that Franklin and Challies were hiding something from him, and that larger forces were at work in trying to get him into the ACF. It almost seemed like a setup, but one he couldn't understand. He saw no way out. He had no real choice.

"Fine." His voice spoke almost without his consent.

Challies mumbled into his Tracker.

"Detainee twenty-eight-thirty-seven is yes. Proceed with Change of Status. Protocol Twelve." Rex turned and looked at the Protector. Challies made eye contact with Rex. The Protector didn't say anything else, but Rex had the impression that Challies was happy with his choice.

Franklin removed his hand from Rex's shoulder. Rex turned to face his foster dad. Franklin's expression seemed relieved.

"These bodies are from below," he said, stepping back. "From Cthonia. They've climbed up the Proboscis and attacked our ACF guards. Now you'll be able to help us find out why they came."

FOUR

FROM THE MORGUE, CHALLIES AND ROMAN walked Rex through the transit tubes to a chamber on the western side of the island. There, Franklin patted Rex on the shoulder and left without a word. It was as if this was what he'd been expecting all along—an outcome that was perfectly natural. Challies ran his Nanokepp Card over the hatch, which slid open. Following Challies's lead and followed by Roman, Rex stepped inside.

Challies pointed to a series of three chairs pushed up against the wall, which was flat and gray. Like all the other rooms in Ætheria, this one was heated, which gave Rex time to massage his arms and legs, bringing warmth and blood back to his extremities.

"Wait here," Challies said, pointing to the chairs. "I'll just be a minute." He paused before stepping back and looked around. "You did the right thing. You know, my brother was . . . Tossed. A long time ago. Before I joined."

"Challies!" Roman snapped, giving his partner a withering look. Challies glanced over and looked back to Rex.

"Okay," he said, the emotion gone from his voice. "Just stay here, alright?" he said to Rex.

Rex nodded and sat. Roman sat next to him, as if they were two family members going to the doctor's together—Rex was the sick one, and Roman was there to comfort him. But the only comfort Rex had was the hope that Roman would soon leave him alone. As they sat, Roman never once looked at Rex or said anything. His eyes remained forward, like some kind of robot whose only job it was to follow orders and not think.

The two were in what looked like an ACF office. Several feet in front of Rex, a large, solid desk rose up from the floor to a height of about four feet, leaving just one foot for someone's head to peek over. An animated ACF clerk sat perched on the other side. A nameplate sat on the nearest edge: Protector Perin. Wearing the same blue uniform as Challies and Roman, Perin shuffled his hands over the desk as if trying to squash invisible but agile bugs. Rex couldn't see what Perin was working with, but he concluded the desk surface must've been some sort of touch screen, and Perin was manipulating data. Every few seconds, his desktop would let out several quick beeps.

Behind him, five other Protectors operated similar desks, but they were much more sedate, staring into space. Only when Perin's desk beeped would one wake up and tickle their desktops with their fingertips. After a few seconds, they would finish whatever it was they were doing and again fall into their catatonic state.

To the clerks' right, a thin aisle stretched off into the distance, opening up into an even wider hallway filled with oval-shaped hatches. ACF Protectors of all shapes and sizes shuffled about, going into and out of rooms, walking up and down the hallway, and coming into and out of the main office.

The only thing that stood out about the agents was they all seemed at least twenty or so years old. There were none older than about thirty. Which made sense, since everyone in Ætheria over thirty was required to work in administrative work running the archipelago. Active duties—policing, maintenance, cleaning, farming, processing food and raw materials extracted from Cthonia—were reserved for the under-thirties. "They're more able at that age," his foster dad had once said. "After thirty, your body doesn't respond the same way anymore. Not a good thing if you're hanging underneath one of the islands trying to repair the support wires."

Rex had no idea where Challies had gone. He waited for more than two hours. One hundred and twenty minutes of watching just as many ACF agents, officers, and clerks buzzing about like bees coming into and out of a hive. Several times Rex felt his eyelids grow heavy, and then his head would jerk or his legs would snap straight, waking him up.

He stretched and stifled a yawn.

From the end of the hallway, Challies appeared and turned in Rex's direction. He was carrying something in his arms—a pile of folded cloth with some sort of device on top.

"Come with me," he said when he reached Rex. Rex stood. His legs tingled with pins and needles. He glanced at what Challies was carrying and recognized a folded AG suit and what looked like a brand-new ACF uniform. UV goggles and a Tracker watch lay on top of the heap. It was the same device all of the ACF Protectors and Ætheria's Council members wore, including Rex's foster dad: black, smooth, faceless, and capable of transmitting the wearer's whereabouts as well as any words they might say.

Rex followed Challies into the hallway. Behind him, Roman's footsteps trundled along.

"Here," Challies said, stopping so suddenly Rex almost ran into him. His hands full, Challies nodded to the door on Rex's right. "Go in here and change. AG suit first, then uniform on top. Sorry, you don't have a badge yet. Or a nametag. You'll get those later, I imagine." He held out the pile of clothing. When Rex took it, Challies snatched up the Tracker and began toying with it, turning it over in his hands. "I'll help you with this when you get out," he said.

Rex stepped into the room, which turned out to be a large but empty bathroom. Rex pulled off the pink shorts, shirt, and flip-flops and crumpled them together in a pile, flip-flops on top. He pulled on the AG suit, sighing as the ultralight insulation finished off the job of warming his frigid body. The only times he'd ever gone without wearing the skintight material was while sleeping at home. Even though the buildings were heated, he still kept it on inside. It was nice again to have his feet comfortably sheathed by the AG suit's integrated thermal booties, which made separate footwear unnecessary. Everything in Ætheria was about efficiency. If the Ætherians could do without it and survive, they did.

This included having an adequate amount of oxygen, which was reserved for Ætherian High Command.

With the suit on, Rex pulled the goggles over his head, but left the lenses high on his forehead, since they were inside. No one in Ætheria could dream of living without these, either. Spend just thirty minutes outside with nothing covering your eyes, and your corneas get fried by the sun. The intense ultraviolet radiation would blind you.

Rex scooped up the pile of cloth and stepped back into the hallway. No sooner had the automated hatch behind him slid shut than Challies had stepped forward and grabbed his left wrist, almost making Rex drop the clothes.

"Hey!" Rex said, steadying his load. Challies did not look up.

"You're right-handed, right?"

"No," Rex said. Challies let his wrist go.

"Oh." He snatched Rex's right wrist instead. "This has to go on your nondominant arm." Challies pulled the watch around Rex's right wrist just tight enough to allow for no wiggle room, but not so tight as to cause pain. Moving quickly and expertly, he clicked the watch's buckle into place and then pulled some sort of key from his pocket. Challies stuck the key into the side of the watch and turned. The watch beeped.

"This is a honing sensor," he said. "A Tracker. All ACF wear them. So does the Ætherian Council. But you probably know that. This way anyone can find you—anyone in the Ætherian Council, that is. Normally you get it after training. But given your, um, circumstance, things are being sped up. So there you go. Look, it has your name and ID number on it."

Rex lifted his wrist and gazed at the device. Across its smooth black surface, REX 1421 was inscribed.

The inscription looked professional, like something that had to be ordered or took time. Rex wondered how long it had been since the inscription had been made.

"Now," Challies continued, nodding towards the main office where Rex had sat. "We need to get you to the others. They're up at Bernuac HQ, toward the northern side of the archipelago. You're late. Of course, you wouldn't have been late if you'd only followed along right away, like we asked."

"Late? For what?"

"The briefing began this morning. For the ACF. But now we need to hurry; it'll take us at least thirty minutes to Zipp there," Challies said, referring to the system of harnessed Zipp lines the Ætherians used to get from island to island. "So good luck. And do the right thing."

Rex wondered at Challies's comments. It would only be days later, when chaos had erupted and Rex's life was in danger, that the reasons for Challies's riddles would come to light.

The room teemed with ACF recruits. When they got to the hatch, Challies pushed Rex in and disappeared, leaving Rex to wonder at his new surroundings.

The room was square and tall: about sixty-by-sixty feet and twenty feet high. Rex was surprised to see no tables, no chairs, no screens, and no one who seemed to be in charge. Instead, groups of five or six ACF recruits sat in clusters throughout the room, talking all at once. But as Rex scanned their ACF uniforms, he soon realized that they were more than recruits: some wore insignias, some wore badges, and some wore utility belts that seemed old and worn. These were experienced ACF Protectors, not recruits. What was he doing here? Not only was he clearly younger than everyone in the room, but he'd been thrown in with a trained group. His face burned as chatter, conversation, and an occasional laugh filled the room with a mind-rattling din.

"Welcome!" a girl's voice blurted over the hubbub.

Rex jumped, startled. Someone placed their hand on his upper arm and squeezed. He turned and saw a woman in her early twenties, her eyes boring into his.

Rex nodded and saw her uniform was different from the others. A small, circular, red patch was affixed to the top center of her chest, right where her breastbone stopped and her neck began. It was like the knot of a bowtie that had drooped. Rex had seen ACF Protectors like her before—or at least with the same red patch. He'd always assumed they had some kind of higher rank than the regular recruits or Protectors, though what exactly he'd never known or cared. She carried a medium-sized black duffel bag in her other hand.

"I'm Yoné," she said. "I'm Point for this unit."

"Unit? Point?" Rex asked.

"Yeah. In the ACF, a group of six is a unit. Six units make up a consort, and six consorts are a team. The Point leads. Here they are." She turned and pointed to five other ACF who'd gathered behind her. They must've been following her. Their eyes were trained on Rex.

"You seem young . . . " one of the others said. "How old are you?"

"Sixteen," Rex said, looking at the man who'd asked the question. He seemed to be in his early twenties. He frowned at Rex's answer.

"Sixteen?" he mumbled. "That's impossible! You have to be eighteen to . . . "

"Quiet!" a voice boomed behind Rex. He turned around and saw Roman glaring at the recruit who'd spoken. Rex gave a start; he hadn't seen the Protector come in, much less sidle up to them. "Not all questions should be asked," Roman said. Rex had the impression that Roman was trying to bore a hole through the recruit with his eyes. Roman held the stare for a moment, before glancing knowingly at Rex and walking away.

"Phil!" Yoné snapped at the recruit as soon as Roman had left. She shifted her eyes to Rex. He wondered if she already knew about his age and, presumably, his "special circumstance," as Challies had put it. Rex wondered how much else she knew. Rex glanced around the room and felt embarrassed at the thought that he was not only the youngest person here, but that everyone else already seemed trained and experienced.

"Forget about age," Yoné continued, "Rex here is new to the ACF, and I'm sure he'll be a great help. Don't you worry about him. He's my responsibility." She turned to Rex. "Since you just got here, why don't we go around and introduce ourselves, maybe? I'm Yoné, but you know that already." She pointed to Rex. "Why don't you start?"

"Rex."

Yoné nodded. She then moved her hand counterclockwise around the circle that had formed, each person saying their name when she pointed.

"Anton."

"Phil."

"Carrie."

"Erla."

"Jon."

"So, before you got here," Yoné continued, her voice booming to be heard over the commotion, "I was explaining the mission we've got ahead of us. Now the rest of you heard this already," she glanced at the five other members of her team, "but just let me go over it again for Rex's sake, I guess." Several heads nodded, their eyes riveted on Rex. Their expressions betrayed their thoughts: he had no business being there.

"The ACF is divided into two main parts. There's the largest part, the Patrol Branch, whose job it is to maintain safety and compliance throughout Ætheria. Making sure people produce, don't waste, follow the rules . . . that sort of thing. If ever you've seen any of us around in Ætheria, these are the ones you've seen. The other branch is the Armed Branch. This part is designed to protect Ætheria from threats from the outside. You've never seen any of them, except for Challies and Roman." Yoné stood up straight and cracked her knuckles.

"Why not?" Rex asked.

Yoné hesitated.

"Until now, they haven't existed. The threats, I mean."

Everyone nodded, but Rex felt a sense of apprehension well up. Threats? What threats? How did those frozen bodies play into all of this? Was she referring to them?

"Aside from the atmosphere," Yoné continued, "there have never been any threats, really. I heard once that when Ætheria was first built, people talked about forming some kind of force, but that never happened. There had been rumors of people left down below, but they were always just rumors. No one ever saw any trace. Not in eight centuries. No word. No warnings. No threats. No fear. So . . . no protection force."

"So why talk about an Armed Branch if it doesn't even exist?" Rex asked. Even though he'd grown up with the fourth most powerful man in Ætheria, this was the first time he was hearing about any of this.

It's not that his foster dad ever gave the impression that he had been hiding things. It was just that Rex had never thought to ask or even wonder about Ætheria's past. As was the case with anyone, you only really start to care about your history when it affects you personally.

"We're the first ones," Yoné said. "In the Armed Branch, that is."

"Now?" Rex asked. "Why us? Why now? Aren't I too young for this? I haven't even received any training. They told me this was training, but that was clearly a lie! And don't you know I was forced—"

"Shhh!" Yoné shot him a look before glancing around as if nervous someone had heard. Rex's question triggered a reaction in the others, who bombarded Yoné with questions.

"Look, I can't say anything about your age," Yoné said. Rex noticed that she was avoiding his eyes. "All I've been told is that you're here, and I'm to work with you. So why don't we focus on what we're here to do? Can we do that? And let's avoid too many questions."

Rex tried to calm himself. He pulled his right hand to his mouth and chewed the edge of his thumbnail. The bulky Tracker irritated the skin under its strap. The members of Yoné's unit looked at her expectantly.

"Last night—or rather, very early this morning—four bodies turned up," Yoné said, raising her hands to calm the questions. "Strange bodies. Frozen bodies. Bodies from . . . below."

Uproar. Aside from Yoné, Rex suddenly felt he had at least one advantage over these trained and experienced ACF: he was the only person here—aside from Yoné—who knew anything about the bodies. And if Franklin hadn't told him about their discovery, Rex wouldn't have even known that. According to his foster dad and Yoné, the ACF had discovered the bodies that morning after some kind of fight between the ACF and the two other Cthonians—a fight that had led to their trial, which was going on right now. People didn't talk about news like that in Ætheria. People talked about other things: the wind, the cold, the crops, the air, school, training, administration. Life was so tough up here, there wasn't much room for rumors and small talk.

Rex turned his head around, scanning the room. He saw other units assembled around other Points. He wondered if everyone was getting the same briefing.

Yoné briefed her unit on the Cthonian bodies. That they'd been discovered only on Tátea and on no other island; that their discovery prompted the ACF to begin searches throughout Ætheria. The searches were still underway, but they hadn't turned up anything yet. And the reason for this seemed simple: whoever these Cthonians had been, they hadn't figured out how to use the Zipp lines. As Rex knew all too well, these were locked down to anyone not possessing Level Black Nanokepp Cards. And the Cthonians could not have had these.

But what was so worrying to the ACF and the

Ætherian Council was that the bodies had appeared on the most restricted island of the entire Ætherian archipelago, which contained the Power Works, the detention and interrogation center, and the morgue. Moreover, the Cthonians had clearly climbed up the Proboscis from below—all thirty thousand feet from below, which was an almost superhuman feat involving atmospheric pressure changes, significant drops in oxygen saturation, and plummeting temperatures . . . not to mention the sheer fatigue that such a climb would effect on someone's arms and legs. Not only that, but, according to Yoné, "It is almost unthinkable to climb up that tube. We only go down it once per month for inspection. And even then, it's extremely tiring and dangerous."

"Why?" Rex asked.

"Well, that's a thirty-thousand-foot climb—or descent—depending on which way you look. Add to that the things I just mentioned and you've got a recipe for disaster. And what's more, the area covered by the Welcans cloud is subject to lightning strikes and dramatic spikes in temperature. The Proboscis isn't grounded, so one strike while someone's in it and you're dead."

"But you said someone goes down every month?"

"A small team does, yes. But then we check the weather and try to find a time when the cloud is calmer."

"Has anyone ever died going down the tube?"

"What do you think?"

Rex's mouth opened as if he wanted to say something, but no words came out.

"Right now," Yoné continued, "the only other place we need to search is down the Proboscis itself. Because that's how they came up. Other ACF have been searching the rest of Ætheria all morning. What we don't know is if there are any more Cthonians down there—in the Proboscis. But I'll get to that."

As if trying to change the topic, Yoné stopped speaking and opened her black nylon bag. She reached in and pulled out what looked like a black metallic football: an oblong object made of four diamond-shaped slices of unpolished material. It looked almost like an abnormally large egg.

"Aside from the bodies, we found this," she said, lifting the thing up and turning it in her hands, "and this is what caused us to grow most alarmed, and what led for us to mobilize so quickly. It was attached to the one of the frozen Cthonian's backs like a backpack. We found three total. One of the others in the Proboscis had a back harness that was empty. We think his pack fell down the tube and may have landed on one of the service platforms farther down, but we don't know. Take a look," she handed the egg to Anton, who sat to her left. His face displayed shock when she released the egg into his hands.

"It hardly weighs anything," he said, passing it around. When it got to Rex, he was also surprised. The thing couldn't have weighed more than an ounce or two. Rex ran his hands over its smooth surface. It felt like stratoneum—the ultralight but extremely strong mineral that formed Ætheria's stilts to Cthonia. Rex passed the egg along and glanced around the room. The other groups were taking turns examining the two other devices. Yoné continued.

"We were able to pry them open," she said. "All of them seem to have been attached to a type of quick-release harness on the bodies' backs. In this one we were able to find this: a message on a microprocessor. We couldn't access anything on the others. The cold had ruined the circuits."

Yoné turned and pulled out a NotaScript from her bag. She turned it on and held it up so that they could all read from the glowing screen. The message was short and written in some kind of garbled language. As Rex studied the text, his blood chilled the more he understood.

PAST make recon o/povr plnt 4 flt struct····

NO how many pple····

povr plnt ❼ O2, El, + H20 4 pple here····suspicions?

❼ ❼ ≈

PROPOSED PRE-EMPTIVE CONTACT:::YES

▽

"What do you make of this?" Yoné asked the group.

"I don't want to be paranoid," Erla said, "but are these spies, do you think?" Rex looked at Erla as she spoke.

"What? Spies?" Rex asked. "But what about the other bodies?" Rex turned to Yoné, who had closed her NotaScript and held it in her lap. "You said they had them as well?"

"That's right," Yoné answered. "But the strange thing is this: we found these things not attached to the bodies' backs, but on the service platform next to them. What we think is that the things were designed to be jettisoned back to Cthonia to transmit messages. We think this because when we caught the two others up top, the packs shot off of their backs when they were dazed. The packs fell over the edge and, we imagine, have been intercepted below. That is, if there are many more Cthonians down there . . . "

The recruits sat for a moment, thinking. The noise continued around them, filling the room. Rex glanced up and saw several Points holding up their NotaScripts, just as Yoné had done. When she had finished with the pack, she walked it to another group who had not yet examined one. They passed it around just as she had done. In this way, each group got to inspect a pack closely, wondering what it meant for Ætheria.

"What else does it mean?" Anton asked in a soothing voice. For once one of the group didn't shout. Rex heard his voice as clearly as if the room were silent.

Yoné's face darkened. "This seems to be communicating information about Ætheria. It also seems to be suggesting some kind of 'pre-emptive contact,' whatever that means. But why now? No one can figure. Why these people . . . these Cthonians? We don't know. Most of us are still reeling from the fact these people actually exist, let alone that they are climbing up to Tátea for some sort of 'contact.' We need to figure out who these people are. We need to understand if there is some kind of society down there, and if they've evolved and changed like this—tall, pale skin, large brains, and whatnot. The bottom line is that we can't ignore it. We've always suspected that there were small groups of survivors scattered around down there. But now we're wondering if there's not more . . . and if they're dangerous.

"Right now the plan is this: There are one hundred and twenty-one recruits in here. We have twenty units. Tomorrow, half of you, Unit Alif, will get a surveillance briefing from Bernuac Headquarters, while the other half, Unit Yā, will start weapons training. In two nights, Unit Alif will descend the Proboscis to try to see if there are any traces of Cthonians farther down the tube. We have to hurry. During this time, units will stay together and work together.

"One thing: we've never been able to see or send radio or radar through the Welcans cloud. The monthly maintenance teams also look around outside and below the cloud, but in eight hundred years all they've ever reported was just empty desert—desert and acid rain as far as the eye can see. Which is why Ætheria was built in the first place: to escape and survive that godforsaken wasteland.

"But now . . . now it looks like we may have been wrong all along."

"Excuse me?" Rex asked.

Yoné glanced at Rex with determined eyes. "Yes?"

"When was the last time someone went below the Welcans cloud for maintenance? What I mean is, when was the last time any Ætherian looked around down there?"

"Just over three weeks ago. We go down at the beginning of each month."

"I'm assuming you saw nothing last time?"

"Nope. Like I said: nothing. Just desert."

"And now . . . why aren't they the ones going down there? Why me?" Rex glanced at the others in his unit.

Yoné glared at him. "Orders. I have orders. I told you that. And remember, not all questions should be asked. You all are in Unit Alif. You're going down tomorrow. It'll be dangerous. Who knows what we'll see? But we have to look."

Rex felt a chill. Yoné's voice seemed more robotic and contrived than before. He had the distinct feeling she was hiding something from him. They all were.

FIVE

WHEN YONÉ HAD FINISHED BRIEFING HER group, the remaining ACF units came together in Bernuac HQ's Assembly Hall. Rex filed into the room and assembled along with the members of his unit.

"Good afternoon, ACF," a woman's voice boomed through the hall's stentrophones, two massive speakers hanging at the front and on either side of a lectern raised up on a stage.

Some sort of officer had stepped up to the podium and was looking over the recruits, her hands behind her back. She wore a uniform similar to everyone else's, the only difference being her badge and insignia nearly covered her entire stomach. Her features were stony, as if chiseled by years of exposure to the howling wind and cold of Ætheria. She looked like someone not to be toyed with. Still, the hint of a smile tickled the corner of her mouth. She looked like a mother beaming with pride for her children, but also someone who didn't want anyone else to suspect that she harbored a soft spot in her heart. Like Roman and Franklin, she wore an oxygen tank and respirator.

"My name is Deputy Head Schlott. I am the Head of the Ætherian Cover Force, and I report directly to the Head Ductor. My job here is to get you ready." She paused and took a deep breath. "Today you will be briefed as reconnaissance Auscultors for the ACF. I know your Points have already explained how important—and how unprecedented—this work is."

A rustle stirred the crowd like a small field of grass blowing in a gentle breeze. Rex turned to Yoné.

"Auscultor? What's that?" he asked.

Yoné leered at him. "Just listen."

"Quiet, please." Schlott began to pace in front of the podium, talking as she did. Rex couldn't see if she was wearing a microphone that projected her voice through the stentrophones—but her voice echoed through the room like that of an opera singer. Like Roman's, her voice was clear, unimpeded by the strains of hypoxia.

"Our main goal today is to give you an introduction to what we are going to be looking at—what we are going to be looking for. As Auscultors, that will be your primary job: look and listen, and gather reconnaissance.

"As the ACF, you need to be reminded of the full story of our world—the one schools don't know and, even if they did, are not authorized to share. You have heard this before, I know, but we must always remember where we've come from. Remembering this will help us remember where we're going. It will also be important to remember that part of our world we need you to take a look at: the part below the Welcans."

A murmur rippled through the crowd. Schlott scanned the units but said nothing. When the noise died down, Schlott continued.

"Now, since you've been in the ACF, you've maintained your fitness through daily exercises and calisthenics. This is good . . . good and necessary. Your bodies must always stay used to functioning with little oxygen. Because, quite frankly, we will be asking that you climb down a very long ladder, look, listen, and then climb back up. Yes, this is danger-ous—dangerous because of the fatigue; dangerous because of the storms that might be outside the Proboscis; dangerous because we don't know if there are any other Cthonians still down there; and dan-gerous because if there are, we don't know what their intentions against us are. But, for our purposes, we have to. And we've learned a lot over the years. We have safety measures. And despite the risk, we have to see how these Cthonians have been coming up.

For our agents can find no other way to answer our questions than to send units of Auscultors down."

Rex looked up, frustration once again churning. Training? He'd never received any training. As for exercise, the lack of oxygen made this all but impossible. Were the ACF more used to the thin air? Had they received special acclimation? He knew that only the High Command had access to bottled oxygen, but was any reserved for the ACF at all?

At the front of the room, Schlott stepped to the side of the lectern and the lights dimmed. The wall behind her came to life. A soft glow began at the edges and worked its way to the center. The wall was also a pelescran. Static flickered across the surface and soft music rose in a minor key. The title, *Ætheria and Cthonia: The Path of Two Worlds*, rose and faded in the pelescran's center.

Despite his growing worry, Rex chuckled to himself. Schlott was showing a documentary. Was that their "remembering"? A movie? Over the next ten minutes, the pelescran danced with images—some real, some digital—of a green and flowering planet; of rivers; of blue skies turning gray and red; of a massive, yellowish Welcans cloud forming twenty thousand feet over Cthonia's surface; of miles-high scaffolding reaching into the stratosphere as Ætheria's construction began eight hundred years ago; of the first completed islands of the archipelago; of Ætheria in its current state of twenty-four floating islands, each held up by six-mile-long stratoneum stilts and guy wires that stretched to Cthonia, disappearing in the swirling, toxic lithium Welcans cloud.

As the images dissolved into each other, a woman's voice narrated. She spoke with some sort of accent Rex had never heard before—one in which she didn't pronounce the final R's in words and in which the A's were much more open than he was used to, as if she were stifling a yawn. Rex glanced around the room. The other recruits faced the screen—most with folded arms. They'd clearly seen this many times before. Rex looked back to the pelescran and let himself be carried through Ætheria's near millennium-long history.

———

"Many hundreds of years ago, the population of Cthonia realized it was in crisis. Over-farming and pollution caused planet-wide temperatures to rise. Incidences of emphysema, allergies, and cancer spiked. People were dying. The environment was dying. Cthonia was being suffocated by people's blindness.

"In 3716 of the Current Era, a small group of visionaries realized that life on Cthonia was doomed. With private funding, they built structures far up in the stratosphere—structures that would be safe from a strange, yellow cloud of toxins forming at about twenty thousand feet of altitude. This cloud would come to be known as the deadly Welcans cloud.

"At first they built three towers, each at an altitude of thirty thousand feet. After stabilizing the towers against gravity and the perpetual winds, they set to generating energy for a complex that was growing—a complex that would soon be known as Ætheria. On Tátea, the southernmost island, a tube—later to be known as the Proboscis—was built to siphon up cthoneum gas, water, and oxygen from the environment below; all of this would then be converted to electricity, potable water, and denser oxygen, which was to be reserved for certain administrative needs in the complex. Building the Proboscis took many failed attempts. Unlike the guy wires and thin stratoneum struts holding up the islands, the Proboscis was racked by the violent storms inside the Welcans cloud. It became clear that a weather- and wind-proof solution was necessary. After four prototypes, the Ætherians succeeded in creating a rigid, impervious form that would not break under the strains of the cloud, and would also draw up the necessary elements from below. Success had been attained, and Ætheria flourished.

"Once Ætheria became energy self-sufficient, its

people turned to food cultivation, and small-scale farming in biodomes was instituted on two new islands. Within the span of three hundred years, Ætheria became a self-sustaining, autonomous colony of survivors.

"Since Ætheria's colonization, the Welcans cloud hugging Cthonia has become so thick that it has rendered all transportation or communication between the Cthonian and the Ætherian spheres impracticable. When the last of the Ætherian settlers left Cthonia, they reported a world in the process of self-destruction: a civil war had erupted among those left behind. The population was dwindling, and in certain places Cthonia's people could not leave their homes without wearing protective respirators.

"That was nearly eight hundred years ago. Since then, Ætheria's top scientists have estimated that not only has the atmosphere below become toxic, but that life forms as they used to be are all but extinct. Rumors have circulated that pockets of Cthonians may have survived and continued their fight for survival with the aid of oxygen respirators. But the reality is that in nearly one thousand years, no evidence of their existence has surfaced, and the atmosphere has proven too dangerous to attempt any sort of sincere information gathering.

"Now, Ætheria is the only hope for humans' survival. Ætheria is Right. Ætheria is Good. Ætheria is Salvation."

———

The pelescran flickered and went dark. The room's lights were turned on. Rex squinted and looked around.

He didn't find the documentary that educational. He felt more like he was being shown some overblown, overly dramatic propaganda film. But maybe that was because his foster dad had already told him most of what the narrator said. Rex wondered if any of the stuff in the movie was news to anyone else in the room.

"Questions?" Schlott stepped back to her spot at the podium. Rex raised his hand. "Yes? In the back?"

"How did the Welcans form?"

Schlott nodded. "Good question. The Welcans is made from fermionic lithium. That's lithium that has reacted at extreme temperatures to produce an impenetrable gas. Any signals, radio waves, sonar, you name it—nothing can get through it when it is so dense. We were lucky to have the Proboscis in place before the concentrations got so thick that it would've been impossible to navigate, even on top of the bad weather, which already made things hard enough.

"The source of the cloud—we think—is from factory production that got out of control in the late twenty-second century CE—the Cthonians had found that supercooled lithium helped in hardening steel for producing airships, guns, and other industrial needs. One day the largest of these factories experienced an O-ring crack in its core, starting a chain reaction that quickly spread beyond the factory.

The Welcans grew and grew until we have what you see now. A yellow, impenetrable, toxic cloud."

A murmur. Nods.

"Other questions?" Schlott scanned the room. Rex raised his hand again. Schlott hesitated. She seemed to be glaring at Rex from the front of the room, but he couldn't be sure. "Yes?"

"Has no one from Ætheria ever tried to explore below? What about survivors? Has anyone ever communicated with them? Because they're clearly there, and that's why we're all here . . . "

A few heads turned and looked at Rex, but when he made eye contact they looked away.

Schlott looked irritated. "You're Franklin Strapp's son, aren't you?" she asked. Before Rex could answer, she pulled her NotaScript from her side and typed something into the touch screen. "A young conscript?"

"Yes."

"Hmm." She finished reading the text on her NotaScript screen and lowered the device. "Good question." Her voice sounded phony. "To answer your first question, for the past four or five hundred years, the only real glimpses people have had outside have been while going out and performing maintenance on the Proboscis, the wires, and the struts that hold up Ætheria. But those reports have only come back with the intelligence that Cthonia is what we thought it was: a wasteland. No plants. No life. A desert. As far as the air goes, you can't go anywhere near Cthonia's surface without a respirator. We might've gotten used to living with little air up here, but down there, forget it. One breath without your mask and you're dead.

"And survivors? Well . . . we really had nothing until last night. And that's what we're here to find out. Because clearly we got something wrong." Rex had the brief impression that Schlott's face flushed at her statement. But she quickly looked back down at her NotaScript screen before continuing.

"So," she said, "if there are no more questions then you should know the plan. From here you will split into two groups—your Points told you this already, I believe." She looked around at the Points scattered around the room. "Those in Unit Alif will head to Room Four down that hall," she pointed to the back left hatch. "And the rest will stay here for now. There you will get your briefing in every-thing you need to make your descent: mask use, air regulation, harnessing, observation and recording techniques . . .

"Because in exactly forty-eight hours, you will divide further into groups of two units each. And from there, you head down the Proboscis to investigate."

SIX

WHEN REX AND HIS UNIT REACHED ROOM
Four, he was surprised to see Challies and
Roman there, arranging a series of compact respirator masks and compressed tanks at the front of the
room. The other recruits and Points filed in and
formed several lines facing what were apparently
their instructors. Challies glanced up and his eyes met
Rex's, but he said nothing. Instead, he and Roman
got right to work lecturing all of the Auscultors on
the proper use of what he referred to as SCRMs—
Self-Contained Respirator Masks—that everyone
would wear for their descent. They then moved on

to the harnesses the Auscultors would be wearing to strap them into the wire ladder—"These will prevent you from falling off in case of turbulence," Challies said—and finally, the photography and recording equipment they were supposed to use to get pictures, radiographs, and sound recordings of anything "noteworthy" that might be happening in the Proboscis below.

"I wonder if anyone will hear you SCRM in one of those," Anton leaned over and whispered to Rex as Roman held one of the masks above his head, tubes dangling like severed, dried intestines.

"Shh," Rex shot back, his face flushing. Since they'd met, Rex had had the impression that Anton had something against him: first expressing disgust at his age, then this. But seeing these masks, Rex was now worried about something else: his claustrophobia. Even wearing the UV goggles at almost all times was sometimes too much for him—not because of the permanent red circles and indents they left in his skin around his eyes, but because just having them on made him feel closed in, trapped. How would it be inside one of those masks, when water vapor from his breath started fogging up the eyepieces, making his head feel like it was trapped in a plastic bag?

Just the thought made his hands go clammy.

When Challies had finished speaking, the Auscultors split into groups of two as he and Roman walked around the room handing out masks.

"These aren't the actual masks you'll be wearing," Challies said, keeping his eyes on the cart of masks he pushed in front as he walked. "These are trainers. So don't worry if you don't see how all the tubes hook up. Because you don't need the air canisters for this part of the training. Your goal here is just to practice putting the mask on and taking it off. Find a partner."

Before Rex could find anyone to work with, Yoné slid up and nudged him in the elbow.

"Hey," she said, looking at him with the hint of a smile in her eyes. There was something new in her expression—something almost empathetic. As if she were trying to make friends, even though she was almost ten years older than him.

"You okay?" she asked. Rex looked up just as Challies shuffled by and plopped a mask onto their table. It made a rubbery thump as the wad of tubes and valves unfurled.

"Oh, wonderful," Rex said. "Just training, like everyone else." He felt self-conscious as soon as the words had left his mouth. He was clearly upset at being thrown into a group of people who already had experience as ACF recruits. He wondered if Yoné caught his sarcasm, but part of him didn't want to offend her. Since they'd met, she'd been a kind presence—he had the impression she sincerely wanted to look out for him.

Avoiding her eyes, Rex picked up the mask and began fidgeting with the tubes. It looked like one big, head-sized bag of rubber that fit over the face, covering the back of the head as well. The eyes bugged out of two slices of metal tubing about a half-inch long. Little rivets held the round glass spectacles in place.

Instead of a breathing hole, the mouth and nose area bulged out as if someone had wedged a small bowl underneath. Three tubes emerged from the mask— two at the mouth area, and one from the back of the head.

"What's this one?" Rex asked, pointing to the head tube.

Yoné reached over and lifted the mask from his hands.

"You know," she said, "I've been trained on how to use one of these but have never actually . . . used it. No need. Other ACF folks have taken care of maintaining the Proboscis as long as I've been here. But . . . " she held up the head tube, "look." She pulled the end of the tube up so that he could see into the end. A network of small, stripped wires dangled from the inside.

"When you wear this and go down, these will be attached to sensors attached to your head and to an intravenous line in your shoulder."

"Intravenous? What?"

"Yeah. To monitor your heartbeat, blood pressure, oxygen saturation, that kind of thing. The intravenous line is to monitor your blood directly, and, if need be, we can give you medication: painkillers and whatnot. Just in case. There's also a wire for your earpiece and mouthpiece. You know, so you can communicate back and forth as you go down."

"Ah." Rex rotated the mask to look inside. He saw one of the tubes ended in a mouthpiece and the other in some kind of smaller adapter. He looked closer. The adapter looked like it was made to fit into the wearer's nose.

"You have to breathe in with your mouth and out with your nose," Yoné said. "Wanna try it on?"

Rex looked around and saw that other ACF were pulling their masks on, pulling them off, or looking around the room from inside. It was as if the room were slowly being infiltrated by some sort of alien soldiers trying to blend in with the rest of the Ætherians but not doing a good job. The thought reminded Rex of the frozen bodies. Had their goal been to blend in?

Their masks had been different, after all. They had only covered their nose and mouth. Why? Why not protect the eyes as well? Perhaps they hadn't realized how dangerous the direct UV light was in Ætheria? But how much did the Cthonians know about the Ætherian world anyway?

With Yoné standing behind Rex to help, he pulled the mask closer to his face. His heart beat faster, and his breathing became more labored. He paused, holding the mask a foot away from his head, and took several slow, deep breaths. He tried to imagine the view from Ætheria out over the Welcans cloud—a view that was open and stretched for miles. He tried to imagine the sun rising into the sky and casting its first burning rays onto his face. He imagined removing his UV goggles and closing his eyes, letting the sun's warmth fill him up.

"Okay, you ready?" Yoné's voice from behind woke Rex up. "Why are you waiting? Is something wrong?"

Rex shook his head instead of answering. But he kept his eyes closed.

"Alright then, let's do this," she said and reached over his shoulders to grab the sides of the mask.

Yoné pulled gently but firmly, guiding the mask up and onto Rex's face. The reek of latex filled his nostrils. The smell made him want to gag, but he tried to recall the image of the sun. Yoné pulled again, and the sweaty edges of the mask latched onto the sides of Rex's face like some life-sucking creature. No sooner had the rubber clamped onto his head than the nose plug slid up into his nostrils as if it had a mind of its own and were some kind of burrowing worm. The mouthpiece dangled limp in front of his mouth. As Yoné pulled the mask up and over, it pushed harder into his lips and butted up against his teeth. Rex's head felt as though it were in a rubber vice—thick layers of cellophane wrapping around his head and squeezing out all of the air.

Rex tried to open his eyes but couldn't. Or maybe he could—everything was dark. The hot, sticky air from his exhalations filled the rubbery space with water vapor and stale breath.

His head spun.

Stars danced in front of his eyes.

His skin went cold.

And then the rock-hard floor slammed up into his back.

———

"Rex? Rex? Are you okay?"

A rush of fresh but rarified air flowed over him, chilling his wet face, neck, and hair.

"Rex!" Someone smacked his cheeks—first one and then the other. Rex opened his eyes. Blinding white flooded his retinas, stinging the backs of his eyeballs and forcing him to squint. Yoné was kneeling over him. Rex was lying on his back. Several dozen other faces crowded behind her.

"Sit up. But take it easy," Yoné said, scooping her arm under Rex's back and lifting. He was surprised at how strong she was. She helped him to a sitting position. Rex breathed slowly and deeply. His entire body tingled as if it had fallen asleep like a leg and was now waking up.

"You passed out," Yoné said. Before Rex could say anything, she turned around to the other ACF who had gathered behind her. "Alright, you all. He's fine. You can see that. Now get back to work."

Yoné stood, leaving Rex sitting. He pulled his hand to his forehead. It was cold and clammy. He didn't feel feverish, but touching his skin felt like touching a dead body. He felt sick.

While Rex sat catching his bearings and reorienting himself, Challies and Roman had reappeared and were chatting with Yoné, who had turned her back to Rex as she spoke with them. Rex looked up. Yoné moved her hands around as she spoke, while Challies and Roman looked down and then at each other, as if trying to communicate without speaking. Yoné seemed adamant about something.

Pushing against the floor with his hands, Rex

worked his way to his feet. The three stopped talking and turned to face Rex.

"How do you feel?" Yoné asked.

"Better."

"Are you claustrophobic?" Challies asked, a tinge of concern in his voice. At the word, Roman and Yoné jerked their heads in his direction.

Rex shrugged. "I've never really cared for small spaces, no," he said. "Airlocks and transit tubes and whatnot. Doctors think it goes back to my botched birth. But I've also never put one of those things on." He nodded toward the mask, which one of the three had placed back onto the table.

"Just give him time," Yoné said, her eyes on Challies. Challies nodded.

"Well, Rex," Challies said, picking up the mask. "You'll need to figure out how to get this thing on, because you have a job to do. And you know there are no malingerers here."

"Malinga-what?" Rex asked.

"Malingerers," Yoné answered for Challies. "People pretending to be sick to get out of work."

"What?" Rex snapped. "I'm not . . . "

"What you're not," Challies interrupted, "is in charge of your own decisions anymore. You're an ACF Auscultor. And that means," he handed the mask over to Rex, nodding at his hands to take it. Rex held out his palms and Challies unfolded the mask. "That means you must learn how to handle all of the duties that are given to you. No matter how challenging. I've told you about this: do the right thing and avoid . . . "

"Do I have to put this on again?" Rex interrupted the Protector.

Challies nodded to Yoné.

"Take it home," Yoné said, as if serving as Challies's spokesperson. "We're going to work on harnessing later. But you need to practice with this on your own until you can get it on and keep it on."

"Home?" Rex said. "I can go home?"

"Yes. We go down in two nights. That's when

your active duty begins." She looked around. "At that point, you'll need to stay here, so get anything you need, personal things, you know? Besides," she nodded to the Tracker on his wrist, "they'll know where you are."

"I see."

"And try to get it on without passing out," Challies added. "And remember: you have a mission you became obligated to complete when you entered the ACF. We don't want any more Tossings."

SEVEN

THE HOUSE WAS EMPTY WHEN REX GOT HOME. Typical. His foster dad usually got off of work much later, often after Rex had gone to bed.

Night was falling when he walked in and tossed the mask onto the couch in the living space. He was exhausted. The last time he was here had just been that morning, but it seemed an eternity. In just fifteen hours, he'd been dazed, arrested, interrogated, recruited, and partially prepped for a descent into the Proboscis. He ran his left hand over the Tracker that clasped his right wrist. Anywhere he went, the ACF would know. He felt watched.

Rex's temples were throbbing, and his head spun from fatigue and stress. He turned the lights and the heat on, which really only warmed things enough for the ambient temperature not to be freezing. He still needed his AG suit.

Rex stepped up to the window and pressed his forehead against the glass. He looked out into the growing dark, massaging the back of his neck with his right hand. He no longer felt sick, but something didn't feel right. He couldn't put his finger on it. Part of him wanted to lie down and sleep. Part of him wanted to escape . . . but he knew he couldn't.

The Tracker bumped the bottom of Rex's nape as he rubbed the base of his neck. He stood up straight, leaving an oval-shaped smudge on the window. He pulled his right wrist in front of his stomach and ran the fingers of his left hand over the Tracker's strap. The device was firmly latched, its smooth, black surface staring back up at him. No lights, no beeps— nothing to indicate that it was anything more than an unwieldy piece of plastic. Rex grabbed its blank face and tried to wiggle it. It held firm, as if it had become part of him, but Rex felt a thin layer of moisture that had formed between it and his skin.

Rex looked out over the yellowish Welcans cloud churning about a mile below. The sun glowed orange and hovered over the horizon. Its rays bounced up from the cloud, creating a dazzling show of reds, purples, yellows, and oranges. Rex shifted his eyes from the horizon to the edge of Tátea, which he could see just fifty yards away. Like a promontory jutting out into a turbulent ocean, it wound out and off into the distance. Ten yards in, the turf path wound around the island's perimeter.

Rex turned and glanced back into the room. It now hummed with a dull orange as the sun descended. In the middle of the burgundy couch, the rubber mask stared back at him with lifeless, empty eyes. It looked like the severed head of an alien. The three tubes lay sprawled out like veins or nerves trailing out of the head's stump. All that it needed for the illusion to be complete was blood.

Rex stepped over and picked it up. He turned it over in his hands and immediately felt the same nausea and clamminess from before creeping in. He looked at the clock. It was almost nine o'clock. Dad would be back soon—or at least he should be back. Right now he was off doing God-knows-what on Tátea.

Rex had to figure out some way to get this thing on without passing out. He lowered the mask and looked around.

At the thought of his dad, Rex turned to his right, where his dad's bedroom was. The door was ajar. Through the crack and in the fading light, he could see cupboard doors next to his dad's bed. Dad's liquor cabinet.

Rex glanced at the clock and then the front hatch. Nothing. No sounds from outside, beyond the constant howl of the wind. He'd have to hurry.

Rex rushed into the room and stepped straight over to the cabinet. The smell of shoe polish and alcohol stung his nose. Rex never knew how his dad could even stand to sleep in here with that reek. He knelt and opened the door.

Eight small, shiny metal flasks sat lined up like metallic ACF sentries. Franklin had organized them by size, from shortest to tallest. Rex had no idea what they were, or how strong they were, but right then he didn't care. He lifted each slowly, testing them for weight. He wanted to pick the heaviest one. Hopefully that way his dad wouldn't notice any difference when he got back into the cabinet. This was the first time Rex had gone into his foster dad's liquor cabinet, though he'd always known it was here. When he'd mentioned it to friends before, they'd wanted to steal some, but Rex had refused. Now he was ready. He needed to relax.

Each of the first five flasks felt half full. When Rex picked them up, their liquid contents splashed around inside, sending a bubbling sound bouncing around their metallic interiors. He set down the fifth flask and lifted the sixth, which was as fat as his fore-arm and about twelve inches high.

The first thing he noticed was that this bottle felt full. But no sooner had he pulled it from its spot than he noticed something wrong with the back wall of the cabinet. Part of it jutted out at the bottom, as if the wall were warped or the wrong size to fit the cabinet frame. Behind the dark brown wood, a sliver of white revealed that something had been jammed there. Something hidden. Something paper.

Rex reached forward and wedged the fingernails of his right index and middle fingers under the slat, which buckled at the pressure. Pulling firmly but slowly, he eased the wooden piece away, revealing a flat, two-inch-wide compartment. Only behind the compartment did the actual solid wood of the cabinet form the furniture's true back. Had the cabinet been made this way? Or had Franklin put this here?

The wood creaked. It splintered. Rex grimaced and paused, not wanting to break it. With the crack now large enough to work his fingers in, he pulled once more. With a pop, the entire slat came loose, revealing what had been hidden behind: a small manila envelope.

Rex set the flask down with a heavy clump and looked around. He froze, listening. Only the sound of the thundering jet stream purred through the house. Rex reached forward and slid the envelope from where it had been carefully tucked.

Rex had never seen the envelope before now. He turned it over in his hand and squeezed gently. He couldn't tell if anything was inside.

With one more glance over his shoulder, Rex turned the envelope back over to its flap and eased it open. He slid his fingers inside and pulled out the contents: a single sheet of paper, folded into thirds. He opened it and saw a handwritten letter. Which was strange, since so few people in Ætheria hand-wrote anything. All communication was electronic. His eyes dropped to the signature: Máire.

Rex's throat stung with the pain of the past when he saw the name. It was his mom. With trembling hands, he read:

Frank,

Thank you. Thank you for taking in Rex, my boy. You can't know what I'm feeling right now. You can't know what it's like for a mother to let go of her child. You can't know. I don't know what's going to happen, but I know I have to leave. If I don't go, Rex will be in danger. I can't have that. This is the only chance. Take care of my baby, my beautiful, beautiful boy. He's already so fragile. He almost died. I hope I'll be back some day. Maybe then things will be better. Maybe then I can know what a family is really like.

-Máire

As he read, Rex clenched his jaw and fought back tears. His eyes stung.

His mother had left when he was only two weeks old. Why, he never knew. He had no memories of her—just vague glimpses of a face, but as he got older he became convinced that these were nothing more than a dream. He also had foggy sensations of her laugh. Her smile. And her playing games with him. Or had he dreamed those as well? Could a two-week-old remember anything?

At the sight of the letter, all the sights, sounds, and smells from back then came flooding back. But were they real, or just imagined?

He couldn't remember his foster dad ever talking about the letter. And his foster dad had never mentioned Rex's birth father's name. Who was it? All Franklin had ever said was that his birth father had died in an accident, and that his mom's work had taken her away. But where? Ætheria was not enormous, but every time Rex had brought her up, Franklin just waved him off, saying, "She's gone." It was only as Rex had gotten older that he began to suspect that it had been something else. Had she been Tossed? Rex had often wondered this, because if not, wouldn't he have run into her? Ætheria contained two thousand inhabitants, so it was possible for someone to hide . . . but his mother? But Rex had never gotten the slightest clue . . . not the slightest trace of her whereabouts.

Was she even still alive?

Rex's breath now came in short gasps as he stared at the letter and wrestled with memories he'd thought were dead. His heart pounded in his ears and his head spun. The house was still quiet.

He turned the letter over in his hand and slipped it back into the envelope. As he worked it in, he noticed something else in the bottom corner of the envelope's folds. He turned the envelope upside down and shook. A small square of white paper two inches by two inches floated to the floor; "Máire" was handwritten on the back. Rex scooped it up and turned it over. What he saw filled his body with a sense of warmth and sorrow.

There, in the palm of his hand, the expressionless face of his mother stared back at him from what must've been an identity picture taken years before. Her hair was chestnut and pulled behind her head.

Her eyes were brown and resolute. Just from the picture, she conveyed strength.

Rex examined the image for what felt like minutes. He brought it closer and farther away, squinting at its details. He tried to make out her musculature beneath her skin. He tried to determine what she might've been thinking when the picture had been taken. For his part, this was the first time Rex had ever seen a picture like this. Digital ones, yes, but never a printed one. Even on Nanokepp Cards, which served as Ætheria's identification badges and keys to buildings and Zipp lines, there was only a magnetic chip and a pixelated code. No pictures.

Had Rex been alive when Máire had had this made? Why had she given it to Franklin?

Looking once more around like a burglar afraid of being caught, Rex stuffed the picture into the front pocket of his ACF uniform, which rested atop his thermal AG suit. Working quickly, he replaced the letter and slid the packet back into its hiding place. He sat there, thinking. He looked back and forth between the manila envelope and the dimly glimmering flasks. He took a deep breath.

And then, with fumbling hands, Rex twisted off the bottle's metal cap and lifted the mouth to his lips. He didn't pause to smell what was inside. He took several deep gulps, which caused his throat to burn and tighten. He spat and sputtered, doubled over in a fit of coughing. Tears dripped down his cheeks. He hacked and spat and coughed. His esophagus and stomach burned, but he felt an unusual warmth spreading through his arms and legs.

Rex's AG suit suddenly felt stifling—hot, even. He took several more sips, but this time took them slowly, easily, allowing the fiery alcohol to slide down his throat. His coughing subsided. He took one more long draught and twisted the cap back onto the bottle.

Rex reached forward to replace the bottle and realized that his head had begun to spin. His vision was clear, but he felt as though he was moving through a fog—a cloud of numbness that was taking over his whole body. He took a breath and stood, holding his arms out to his side for balance. He looked up and turned toward the living space. Through his foster dad's bedroom door, he could see the mask still lying on the couch. He took a deep breath, swelling his lungs as much as he could in the hypoxic air. His ribs seemed to crackle under the new pressure.

His fear was gone.

Realizing this, Rex strode into the living space, picked up the mask, and smiled. With visions of his mother dancing around him, he pulled the mask to his face and worked it over his head. The nose plug slid into his nostrils, and he opened his mouth to work in the mouthpiece. The sound of the wind disappeared as he stretched the rest of the mask over the top and back of his head like some oversized swimming cap. With a snap, he let go of the mask.

Rex looked around. Despite the apparent smallness of the eye openings, he was surprised to find he had a clear view of the entire house. This was because the edges of the goggles were lined with some sort of flexible prisms that allowed him to see almost in all directions. He stood up straight and looked around again. The room was growing dark. Mom was gone. Dad was still not home. Rex was alone. But he now had her face to hold on to.

I can do this, Rex thought.

EIGHT

THROUGHOUT THE FOLLOWING TWO DAYS, REX and the other ACF recruits trained at Bernuac HQ, mostly practicing putting their masks on and off, harnessing in and harnessing out, taking digital pictures, and making long-distance recordings. After that night at home, Rex could pull the mask on without many problems. Each time he'd try to remember his mom's face, or he would see the letter, and in one movement he'd yank the mask over his head. Once he got over the initial queasiness of being inside the latex head cover, he was more or less okay. To hold his fears at bay, Rex would focus on whatever was happening around him—or at least whatever he could see through the eye sockets. In spite of his fears, part of Rex was jittery for another reason. They would be given their own oxygen canisters for their descent.

It was decided that the Auscultors would begin the climb down Monday night at 2100, just when the sun was disappearing. According to Yoné, this was because they thought a nighttime descent would provide the cover of darkness in case anyone was down there looking up. Even though the Proboscis was made of opaque stratoneum, she explained, there were access windows every half-mile.

"Why?" Rex asked.

"For maintenance. When they slide down on the wires outside, this lets them look in."

"I have another question," he said. "This just occurred to me."

"Yes?"

"Why is it actually that we have to climb? Why

not lower a camera on a wire? A scope, or something like that?"

Yoné hesitated. "The simple answer is, we don't have a wire long enough. The Proboscis itself is made in sections. It's not one big piece of stratoneum. Same thing for the guy wires and struts. They hook up to others every hundred yards or so."

Rex nodded.

"So," Yoné told her unit as she finished briefing them that afternoon, "our full descent should take at least ten hours. By the time we reach the lower levels of the Proboscis, the sun will have come up."

The members of Yoné's unit nodded. Yoné was already fully clad in her Auscultor gear: an AG suit covered with padded knees and elbows. A small, lunchbox-sized oxygen container clung to her back, its tubes dangling at her side, waiting to be plugged into her mask, which she held in her left hand. She wore a climbing harness and, on top of this, a thick utility belt with several items clipped on: a knife, a flashlight, a radio responder with wires snaking up to her collar, and a strange black handle jutting out to the side.

"Any questions?" Yoné looked them over. Her eyes rested on Rex. He shook his head slightly. He thought he saw the hint of a smile cross her lips. No one raised their hands.

"Good. We'll be going down unit by unit. Ours will be the third in line. Units Alif and Tabé will start first. Each unit will serve as a sort of backup for the others . . . in case something happens."

"What do you think could happen?" Anton asked.

"Well," Yoné said, drawing herself up to her full height as if flexing her muscles. "We have three main concerns. The first is breathable air. Once we get below the Welcans cloud, the air becomes toxic. Even at higher altitudes in the Proboscis, the toxic air can drift upward and kill you. That's why it has oxygen intake vents above the clouds. But your canisters should take care of the air. Each one contains enough compressed oxygen and nitrogen to supply you with a solid week's worth. Well enough to go down and come up.

"Other than that, falls are possible. They've happened in the past when people were building and maintaining the Proboscis. That's why we have these harnesses. You are not to take one step onto any of those ladders without being fully clipped in. We might get banged around some, but, in theory at least, no one should fall." She lingered on her last words.

"Finally, we could encounter hostile elements on the way down."

"Hostile elements?" Rex asked.

"Those bodies—they all came up through the Proboscis. None of them were armed, but they were huge and very strong . . . " Yoné placed her hand on her belt. "Each Point is carrying a Stær gun. And we've been trained to use it."

Rex eyed the device clipped to her belt. He recognized it as the same device Roman had used to daze him two days earlier. Then, he hadn't examined it closely, but now he saw it was black—apparently made of metal or stratoneum and plastic—and part of it jutted out from its case like a handle. The other half was hidden in a black AG case that hugged Yoné's thigh.

"The Stær gun is a," Yoné paused, "a tool that sends out electrically charged wires that will jolt anything they hit with one hundred thousand volts."

"What happens if you get hit with one?" Rex asked, though he knew the answer only too well.

"You are instantly incapacitated."

———

Evening approached. Everyone at Bernuac HQ was tense. The Auscultors had been advised that the risk level for the operation was "high." Rex was on edge.

"You okay?" Yoné surprised Rex. He turned and faced her. She had clipped her facemask to the feeder tubes. It now rested on her shoulder, clipped down by a long epaulet.

"Yeah. Fine," he said. "Just thinking."

"Nervous?"

"Not so much," Rex lied. He ran his hand over his pocket, trying to feel the picture's shape inside. With his gloves on, all he could sense was the wrinkles in his uniform's fabric. A terrified thought struck: what if the picture had fallen out as he was coming back to Bernuac HQ from his house? If not, what if it falls out during the descent? He didn't want to check for it now in front of Yoné, but he decided to move it to one of his AG suit's inside pockets when he had the chance. They were tighter and more secure.

"Let's check you out," Yoné said, grabbing Rex's shoulders and turning him around. He could feel her hands dancing up and down his back, checking his harness, his respirator tank, his utility belt. She snapped the respirator buckles even tighter, causing his body to jerk to the right. She patted him down once more and spun him around to face her.

"Belt, good. AG suit, good. Tracker, good." She

paused and looked him in the eye. "I know your dad, you know. Your foster dad, I mean."

"Ah. Is that why you are taking such good care of me?" Rex held back a smile.

"You'll be fine." She ignored his question.

He said nothing—just stared into her black irises. "Thanks. It wasn't quite my plan to become a spy this fast, you know. I had just a year left of school."

"Spy? Who said anything about being a spy? You're just an Auscultor—your job is to listen. To observe. You can do that. And guess what? It's not like your life is over or anything. Be patient. Give it time. And for now, just do what you're told and things might not be as bad as you think."

"Can I ask you something?" Rex furrowed his brow and stared at Yoné.

"Shoot."

"Doesn't it bother you that I have no training? That everyone here's older than me? Hasn't it occurred to you that here you are, taking me down, and I've only come here two days ago? Aren't you worried? Can't you get me out of this? Is the Ætherian Council trying to get rid of me or something? Is that it?"

"Stop!" she cut him off again, but she looked stricken. "Just trust me. There's a lot you don't know. Things are happening behind the scenes. I can see how you would think things . . . maybe not things like that, but . . . let's just say that people are watching you. Do a good job here today, and who knows how this might end. Nobody wants anything to happen to you. I can't say any more than that."

She held Rex's gaze for a second, until a piercing whistle shot through Bernuac HQ. Rex jumped and looked up, his mind buzzing with Yoné's cryptic words.

"Here," Yoné snapped. "Time to put this on." She reached over and lifted Rex's mask from his left hand. He took a deep breath and concentrated on his mom, her letter, and the burning sensation of the alcohol. But now, Yoné's words fought for control of Rex's mind. What did she mean, people were watching him? Who? His foster dad? Someone else?

In one smooth movement, Yoné pulled Rex's mask up and over his head as if she'd had years of practice doing it. The mask slid into place, the nose plug and mouthpiece finding their mark without Rex's even having to try to grope around for them. The whole apparatus squeezed his head firmly, like two giant hands trying to lift him up by the head. She reached for his belt and unfastened his headlamp, reattaching it to the front of his mask—right above his eyes and in the middle of his forehead. She clicked the side of it, and a piercing beam of white made her face glow in a surreal way. All around the room other headlamps clicked on, making the Auscultors look like a dancing human constellation.

Yoné swiveled behind Rex and began attaching the hoses and vitals monitors. He heard two soft clicks, and suddenly his lungs inflated with the freshest, purest, most concentrated air he'd ever breathed. His chest swelled, and immediately he felt every pore, every vein, every capillary swell. He felt great clarity and strength, as if he'd been injected with some sort of performance-enhancing drug. These were the powerful effects of breathing oxygen. But why couldn't everyone in Ætheria have these? Then, maybe, Ætherians could move faster than a walk and not get dizzy. Then, maybe, Ætherians wouldn't get sick as much. Then . . .

"Units Alif through Xā, formation!" a familiar voice boomed through the stentrophones. Rex looked up and saw Challies pacing at the front of the room. Roman stood off to the side near a wider hatch that was closed. Both men had Stær guns strapped to their waists.

At Challies's order, everyone lined up. Each unit of six formed two lines of three, with their Point at the front. The six units then recreated this formation on a larger scale. Challies and Roman positioned themselves at the front. Yoné slid up to Rex's right. He watched her take position. Catching his gaze, she nodded. He nodded back.

"Auscultors, forward!"

The group advanced, each walking at a natural rhythm. At this point, they weren't fighters, just Auscultors. According to Yoné and Roman, Unit Alif's armed training would only happen once they'd returned with any intelligence from below. Rex wondered if he'd get to use a Stær gun.

When they reached the hatch leading out, they shifted position to fit through the door and down the transit tube. The group now walked two by two, with the only exception being the Points, who walked in between each unit like links in a human chain.

Rex stepped into the tube. He noticed he was breathing normally, and he wasn't feeling dizzy or lightheaded. As long as he kept his eyes on the person's head in front of him, his mind didn't wander. With their masks on, all he saw was a series of bobbing, rubber forms, like an army of playing balls attached to robots' shoulders.

No one talked. The Auscultors followed the Points through the tubes until they reached the limits of the island. There, the last external hatch slid open, allowing a rush of outside air to sweep in and cause each recruit to waver one or two inches. Because the tubes weren't heated and they were all wearing their AG suits, Rex didn't notice any change in temperature—just a blast of the howling jet stream. The group faced southeast—towards Tátea.

About fifty feet ahead, the first unit stepped out of the tube and onto the border path circling the island. The rest waited. Even though no one spoke, Rex knew what was happening. The Auscultors and the Points were crossing two by two on the Zipp lines over to Tátea.

Every minute, the ranks took a step forward. Everyone remained silent, and the Points turned to wave the recruits through. Everything must've been going smoothly. Rex wondered what they'd find in the Proboscis. More bodies? Nothing? Or perhaps a group of armed Cthonians raging upward for a fight? He shivered.

After about twenty minutes, he reached the outlet

hatch and stepped outside. No sooner had his body left the tube than the jet stream threatened to push him over. A hand caught his left shoulder and helped him stand straight up. He looked up and recognized Yoné's uniform, even though her face was hidden behind her mask. Static snapped into Rex's left ear.

"You got this, Rex." It was Yoné. She was transmitting through her radio into Rex's earpiece.

"Thanks. Let's do this."

Rex couldn't make out any facial expressions through her mask, but Yoné nodded to her left, Rex's right. He turned his head and saw Challies standing at the Zipp line platform—a small landing and launching pad to allow people a clean start and stop to their crossings between islands. He was checking each Auscultor's harness as they stepped off the pad and over the expanse, their lives dangling by a taut wire and a pulley that drew them across. Challies waved Rex over. At Challies's waist, the hilt of his Stær gun wiggled like a useless appendage. Rex stepped up, holding his hands out to steady himself. More static.

"Here!" Challies's voice screeched through Rex's earpiece, making him wince. Challies reached over and clasped his hand onto Rex's right shoulder, pulling him around with his other hand. Challies stretched up and pulled the Zipp line harness to Rex's waist. As Challies hooked him in, Rex kept his eyes straight ahead on Ætheria's Power Works, which gripped the side of Tátea. Metal carabiners clicked and Rex's torso jerked slightly. Tátea was more than fifty yards away, and the light was beginning to fade. From this distance, Rex could see the massive Proboscis reaching down from Tátea's southern lip . . . down toward the churning Welcans cloud below and Cthonia beyond.

"Alright, Rex, set!" Challies slapped Rex on the shoulder and walked behind him to the platform. Rex glanced to his left, and Challies gave him a double thumbs-up before stepping back.

The Zipp line pulled at Rex's harness and lifted

his feet off the ground. He gulped, but before he could process what was happening, he was dangling thirty thousand feet above Cthonia with nothing but a quarter-inch-wide wire holding him up. Rex looked down and watched the yellowish Welcans cloud a mile below. From this height, it was hard to make out exactly how big the billows were in relation to the islands of Ætheria, but Rex tried to imagine the shapes, shadows, and constantly roiling nebulous forms morphing into his mother's face. He looked for her in the Welcans and pretended she would appear there, as some sort of giant specter, supporting Rex and encouraging him in what he was about to do. The harness vibrated against his waist as he was pulled over the expanse. He clutched the safety cords with both hands and kept his face downward. The cloud becoming hypnotizing.

Rex closed his eyes. With her face clearly in his mind, he tried to remember her smells, her voice, her touch. But it wouldn't come—none of it. All that danced through his mind's eye was his foster dad's face telling him to do this, to do that, to hurry, and above all not to ask too many questions. *But Mom, Mom, what happened to you? Where are you?*

Rex's lower legs collided into the smooth arrival ramp on Tátea, snapping him from his thoughts. He looked around and saw that Yoné had positioned herself at his arrival just as Challies had done for his takeoff.

Static.

"Rex, come on! Move!" Challies shouted through Rex's earpiece. Rex jerked his head back toward the others and fumbled with his legs to stand and hop ahead and out of the way of the next Auscultors coming over. His fingers danced down to the carabiner to unhook it and drop onto Tátea's surface.

Unhooked, Rex stepped away from the Zipp line landing platform and took his place within his unit. They stood for another thirty or forty minutes while all the Auscultors finished filing over. To keep his claustrophobia from surging again, Rex tried to focus on his mother's face.

Static.

"Points, report!" Challies's voice shot through Rex's earpiece. One by one, the Points answered, speaking in order and going down the line of units.

"All present!"

"All present!"

"All present!"

"All present!"

"All present!"

"All present!"

"Good, follow me!"

Rex couldn't see him from his position, but he knew Challies had made it over and was heading toward the Power Works's service hatch—precisely where the bodies had been found the day before.

That's where they were going to enter the Proboscis and begin their descent.

Just as with the Zipp line, the Auscultors waited and stepped forward as the others entered and disappeared below, one by one, unit by unit. They waited and stepped forward, waited and stepped forward, waited and stepped forward, until Rex's unit reached the hatch.

By now the sun had disappeared behind the western horizon, but the sky still glowed red and orange. The group looked silly, standing there in their masks and headlamps, neither of which were necessary right then. But Rex knew the lights were about to prove vital, and once they crossed the Welcans cloud a mile below, they wouldn't be able to live without their masks.

Three rows ahead of Rex, Yoné stepped up to the service hatch and seemed to be exchanging some words with Challies, who knelt beside the hole. Yoné nodded. She turned back to the rest and raised her right hand. She extended her index finger and swung it in a circle. She turned and disappeared down the hole.

The first three rows did the same, but without turning to signal to the others.

It was Rex's turn.

He stepped up to the service hatch. Its colors had

become monochromatic in the fading light. Challies looked up at him through his goggles.

Static.

"Alright, in you go," Challies said. Rex knelt and put his hands on the edge of the hatch. The inside was pitch black, with only the twirling white head-lamps of the first three units hinting that anything other than death waited below.

Challies reached out and grabbed Rex's hand, making him jump.

Static.

"As soon as you get in, there will be a platform," he said. "Once you're on it, you'll see the ladder. That ladder goes straight down six miles. Do not get on the ladder before you hook in."

"Hook in?" Rex said. "Where?"

"There's a thin wire that runs down the side of the ladder," Challies continued. "Just like we did in training. You clip onto that the wire. Remember, though, every twenty feet you have to unclip to get your carabiner past the support strut. Before you unclip, you must clip your other carabiner to the ladder's rung. This way there's no way you can fall. This is even more important as you get tired. And you will get tired. Your Point has orders to stop every twenty minutes to rest. The harness and carabiners are strong enough to support your weight, so you can take a load off your feet."

Rex nodded and looked down.

"What happens if we find someone?" he asked.

"A Cthonian, you mean?"

"Yes."

Challies took a deep breath and hesitated. He seemed to be deciding what to say. "We'll see. The Points are armed, and as far as we know, the Cthonians are not. Remember that. Just follow their lead."

Rex nodded. He looked down into the darkness and imagined seeing an army of ghost-like Cthonians swarming up at him. But all he saw was the few white dots of the others' headlamps.

"Good luck. This is the easy part." Challies slapped him on the back.

With that Challies lowered Rex into the Proboscis, placing his feet on the exact spot where the three bodies had been recovered two days before.

NINE

REX'S FEET LANDED ON THE FIRST PLATFORM with a dull, metallic thud that he felt more than heard. Once he was in, the pressure of the wind ceased as if it had been switched off. With the open hatch just above his head, the wind still howled like a massive flute. This high-pitched squeal reverberated with overtones of colossally deep rumbling. Darkness squeezed in from all sides.

Rex looked around. His wheezing, almost mechanized breathing hissed in a steady rhythm. His headlamp cast a stinging white circle everywhere he looked. Outside of the ring of light, darkness pushed in, suffocating. From his perch, he could see that the inside of the Proboscis looked like a massive, twenty-yard-wide tube stretching down, down, down, like the throat of some great whale. Rex's breath came in shorter bursts.

Static.

"Stop stalling, get a move on!" Challies's voice rang in Rex's earpiece.

"Okay, I'm going," he answered half-heartedly. He took another deep breath and kept his eyes forward.

In front of him, the black rungs of the Proboscis ladder glowed gray in the beam of his headlamp. Just to the right of the ladder, a smaller wire ran parallel. He looked down and saw that the ladder disappeared through a yard-wide, circular gap in the metal grating. He stepped forward and clipped his right-hand carabiner to the wire. He reached forward and grabbed onto the ladder with his gloved hands. Because the AG insulation was so powerful, he had no sense of the metal's temperature, but he knew at this altitude and with these ambient temperatures it must've been about minus thirty or forty degrees. He glanced down. The others' headlights were becoming smaller and smaller as they descended. Rex tried to imagine what the fall would be like if any one of them were to slip free of their safety equipment. If someone tried to climb down this ladder unharnessed, one slip would send them falling down this tube for six straight miles—not considering how many times their plunging body would crash into the sides of the metallic Proboscis.

"Go!" Challies screamed from above, his voice splitting over the static.

Rex looked up one last time at the hatch and the sunlight beyond, which by now was no more than a faint glow. He looked back down.

He put his foot on the first rung and started down.

Step, step, step, step . . . as Rex worked his way down, he realized that until now he'd never climbed a ladder before—up or down. Because the buildings on Ætheria lay low to the islands they were attached to, there was no need.

Step, step, step, step . . . he moved slowly, carefully, sliding his gloved hands over the outside of the ladder, but sustaining enough pressure to hold his grip. With each step, he felt the small metal rungs push into his AG booties and cause the soles to arch as he placed his weight on each foot.

Step, step, step, step . . .

Ka-clunk.

Rex's harness carabiner rattled against the first safety wire support. The sound sent a wave of adrenaline through his body. His neck grew moist and his heart rapped in his chest. Even though there were other ACF Auscultors and Points in the Proboscis with him, he was terrified that any noise he made would alert hidden Cthonians below of his presence. What would they do if they were there? Attack? Retreat? Try to talk? Rex had never seen people as large as the Cthonians in the morgue. Surely they were much stronger than any of the Ætherians. And weapons? The Ætherians had their Stær guns, but what sort of weapons did the Cthonians have? And would they use them? Challies had said they were unarmed, but how did he know?

Moving inch by inch, Rex looked down and grabbed his secondary carabiner with his left hand and latched it to the rung just opposite his stomach.

Ka-CLANK! The metallic crack echoed through the Proboscis and sent vibrations up and down the ladder's sides and into Rex's feet and right hand. Terror shot through his body. He yanked at the secondary harness to make sure that the carabiner was secured. Feeling the resistance, he grasped the ladder with his left hand and reached over with his right to shift his primary carabiner around the wire support. It snapped into place. The wire vibrated again. Rex tested the connection. Seeing it was secure, he unhooked his secondary carabiner and continued down.

Step, step, step, step, step, step . . .

After about ten minutes, Rex became aware of a

sensation entering his feet and hands. Beginning deep in the soles of his feet and the palms of his hands, it began as a dull, almost numb pressure, but one that grew and grew with each rung and each step. The rungs soon seemed to take on a life of their own. Each time his feet or hands touched them, the pressure morphed into an ever-increasing, sharp, crushing pain that spread from his feet to his ankles, shins, and knees. Each of his fingers began to scream from the effort of gripping, gripping, gripping, clipping, re-clipping, unclipping, gripping, gripping, and climbing. Rex gritted his teeth against the rhythmic throbbing, which soon distracted him from his initial fear of the Cthonians.

Static.

"Unit Three, halt," Yoné's voice crept through Rex's earpiece. "This will be our first rest stop. There's nothing up ahead. Just dark. No sign of any Cthonian elements. Remember to sit down into your harnesses during these to take the weight off of your arms and legs. They're made for that."

Rex stopped. His legs and arms tingled as if he were still moving down this agonizing descent. Keeping his hands on the ladder's sides to steady himself, he inched down into his harness, which was as sturdy as a chair. Rex eased all of his weight into it and let his feet slip forward off of the rungs. They dangled in the air, while Rex steadied his body.

Static.

"Everyone okay?" Yoné asked. Rex looked down and made out one headlamp about fifty feet below that was pointed up and circling around like a spotlight. Six other lights hovered in between. Yoné was looking up.

"My legs are killing me," Rex answered. As if to convince himself, he tried to flex his feet and groaned as needles shot through his calves and thighs.

"Hmm, already? How bad on a scale of one to ten?"

"What do you mean?"

"One means it doesn't hurt. Ten means you can't take the pain, it's so much. Where's your pain level?"

Rex shook his head. "Seven."

A pause.

"Okay," she continued. "Go ahead and press your sensor. Once. The one on your left shoulder."

"Why?" Rex asked.

"Just do it."

Steadying himself against the ladder, Rex reached his right hand across his chest and pressed the button. Before he could replace his hand onto the ladder, a strange feeling of warmth spread through his body, with the warmest part radiating from the intravenous line. The warmth flooded through his arms, his chest, and his legs.

As Rex moved, he realized his pain had vanished. Not only had it gone, but his legs felt rested, strong. One by one, Rex opened his hands and clenched them into fists. Just as with his legs, all pain had left his hands, his forearms, and his shoulders.

"What was that?" Rex asked.

"Ibumorphide," Yoné answered. "The strongest painkiller there is. You just got point-one cc."

"How much is that?"

"That's like two drops. Almost nothing. But enough for now."

"Wow. Thanks." Rex took a deep breath and worked his arms, hands, and feet. The pain had evaporated.

"Alright, Unit Three, two minutes," Yoné said.

"How far have we gone?" Rex asked.

"Since the hatch?"

"Yes."

"About a half mile. We're halfway to the Welcans cloud."

Halfway to the Welcans cloud. Rex's mind spun at the thought. The billowing, toxic cloud he'd seen so many times in his life was now growing closer than he had ever been before—than most anyone in Ætheria had ever been, aside from those who maintained the Proboscis and the wires. Rex reached up and gripped the front of his mask with his right hand and tugged gently. He could feel the vacuum it formed against the sides and back of his head. It was on tight. He took a deep breath—more to check his equipment than because he needed more air. The oxygen was flowing. Rex listened. Beyond the mask and beyond the sides of the Proboscis, the steady rush of the stratospheric wind moaned against the cylindrical stratoneum. He couldn't detect any difference in sound than what he'd heard at the top—nothing to indicate they were nearing the Welcans cloud. But he knew how violent things would become outside once they neared the toxic clouds. Back at Bernuac HQ, he'd been given even more details about how the cloud allowed for no radio transmission, how it was constantly split by lightning, and how winds inside sometimes gusted at more than one hundred miles per hour. He'd also been told how strong stratoneum metal is, and how since its construction the Proboscis had never succumbed to the pressures from outside . . . how the stratoneum had always held up against the weather . . .

Static.

"Okay, let's go!"

The team continued their descent.

Without speaking, without making any other noise than that of their carabiners racketing against the safety wire, the six units went down, down, down into the darkness of the Proboscis—into the uncertainty of whatever lay within the deadly Welcans cloud.

A rumble. A groan. A whistle. The sounds on the other side of the Proboscis walls grew as if a storm had appeared on the horizon and then swooped down upon them in a fury. Rex paused in his descent, his nerves on edge. No, he hadn't imagined it: the ladder was trembling. At least his hands and legs weren't hurting any more.

And then something changed . . . something inside his mask. The quality of the air he was breathing shifted. The bottled oxygen no longer smelled clean and pure. It smelled off, different, foul even.

"Yoné?"

"Yes?"

"Do you smell that?"

Her form below froze. Rex saw her rotate her head to the side as if smelling the air. But he knew that, like him, all of her air was being filtered into her nostrils through her SCRM mask. She paused. From Rex's point of view, she was only a silhouette surrounded by the other dancing lights from the rest of the team.

Static.

"I smell something, too," someone else chimed in. Rex didn't recognize the voice.

Static.

"There it is," Yoné said. "I smell it."

"What is it?" Rex asked. By now the smell had grown stronger. It was pungent and powerful. It seemed to fill his mask, as if the smell were being pumped in on purpose . . . pumped in to suffocate him. He could still breathe normally, but the smell now caused him to gag—so much so that he tried to breathe through his mouth instead of his nose. Because of the nose plugs, though, this was impossible.

It was the smell of something rancid.

Static.

"I've never smelled that before," Yoné said. Rex saw her head looking around, her light bouncing off of the inside walls of the Proboscis and ladder. "Take a look. Do you see anything? Unit Two! Unit One!" She called out to the teams below them.

"Donny here, Point Unit One!" came the reply. It was followed by another.

"Seán here, Point Unit Two!"

"Are you smelling that?"

"The rotten stuff?"

"Yes."

"Yes, we've picked it up."

"Do you see anything?"

"No, nothing yet. But we're keeping an eye out."

There was a pause.

Static.

"There's something else," Anton's voice echoed through the team's earpieces.

"What is it?" Yoné asked.

"Do you feel that? That wind?"

"What wind?"

As the two spoke, Rex tried to hold his body still. What wind was Anton referring to? He could clearly hear a roaring wind outside the Proboscis. Is that what he meant? But wasn't that normal?

"There's a breeze inside. Something's blowing around inside the Proboscis."

"What? How? Except for vents up top, the Proboscis is sealed. There would have to be an opening below for there to be any draft," Yoné snapped back.

"We don't know. Yet." Anton paused. "We're going to keep moving forward. But we're slowing down. Something's up . . . Something's . . . wrong. Scan all surfaces as you move. We don't want to be surprised."

A breeze inside the Proboscis? Rex tried to hold his body as steady as he could. Because the AG suit's insulation was so powerful—despite the suit's thinness and flexibility—it made it difficult for the wearer to sense wind or moving air. Back on the exposed portions of Ætheria's islands, the only clue you'd have that there were sixty-mile-per-hour winds was the fact that the wind pushed against you like some giant, invisible hand. And now? Rex felt nothing . . . just the overpowering smell that was leaching into his mask.

Static.

"Unit Three, you heard him. Keep your eyes on everything. Take your time. Report any irregularities."

The earpiece clicked silent.

Rex continued down. But instead of descending regularly and with uninterrupted steps, Rex paused at each rung and looked around. His headlamp painted the Proboscis's inside with a glaring white circle interrupted by the irregular forms of smaller pipes, bolts, wires, anchors, and stratoneum joints of the Proboscis walls that extended up and down in either direction. He didn't know what he was looking for, but nothing seemed unusual about what he saw.

Step, look, step, look, step, look. He continued his descent.

With every few rungs he passed, he noticed two things: the smell became stronger, and he became hotter. Within the AG suit, he could feel pools of sweat forming under his armpits and rivulets coursing down his forehead and fogging up the inside of his mask. His back felt wet, and his palms and fingers slid inside the insulated gloves. Outside of the Proboscis, a thunderous roar reminded him that he must've now entered the Welcans cloud itself. Rex looked around. He hoped that if the wind picked up, the structure would hold. But surely they thought of that when they built this thing, he thought, trying to convince himself. That's what they'd said in that film. And then a second thought struck: he was warmer because they were getting closer to Cthonia and farther away from the frigid stratosphere where he'd spent his entire life. He'd never felt heat like this before. For the first time since he'd entered the

Proboscis from up above, he felt like he was stepping into some other, strange world.

"Ugh," he groaned, fighting off the urge to gag. The stench had become overpowering. The air inside his SCRM mask seemed thicker with the reek of whatever he was smelling.

Static.

"What is it?" Yoné asked. "Rex, is there something wrong?"

Rex shook his head to try and shake away both the smell and the sweat that was covering his face.

"Nothing. It's nothing," he said, blinking hard. "It's that smell."

And then he felt it. Something was brushing against his back. It felt like a giant snake crawling over him, or as if someone were pulling off his AG suit. His terror spiking, he spun his head around. The white light of his headlamp revealed only bolts, rivets, and pale sheets of stratoneum.

"What's going on up there?" Yoné asked, her voice urgent.

Rex looked down and straight into her headlamp. She was facing upward. He squinted against her light and looked around once more. The sensation struck his back again and did not abate. It was a steady pressure, like someone stroking his back. And then he realized what it was.

"Do you feel that?" He asked. "I think I feel air . . . some kind of gust pushing up through the Proboscis."

"Yes," Yoné answered. "It's coming from down here. We've . . . "

"Units Two and Three!" someone's voice blared through Rex's earpiece, cutting off Yoné. The voice was panicked. "Come quick! We've found it!"

The dozen or so headlamps that had been dancing around the darkness of the Proboscis suddenly snapped downward, all looking in the same direction. Rex craned his neck and tried to lean out away from the ladder as far as he could reach. All he could see was a group of five or so Auscultors about thirty yards down. They seemed to be gathering together around something. But how? Rex then wondered if they'd reached another platform and were unhooking from the ladder.

"What is it?!" Yoné snapped in reply. Her silhouette had already begun to descend faster. Rex's heart began to thump in panic. He looked up and saw the other Auscultors bearing down on him. He stretched his feet out again and again for the rungs, his arms once again beginning to ache from the effort of moving faster. He tried to look down the ladder as he descended, his gaze and light directed down his stomach and through his arms and legs, which worked mechanically on covering the distance to the others. The ladder's rungs rushed by like a road he was flying over.

"Come quick!" was all the voice answered. *Why is he not telling us what he's found?* Rex wondered. Were there Cthonians heading up at them through the dark? Rex tried to interpret what was going on from the urgency in the Auscultor's voice. He sounded alarmed, terrified even, but more of something he'd

found, as opposed to something that required immediate action . . . or immediate retaliation.

Faster and faster Rex went down. The stench
stung his nostrils and the heat was becoming almost
unbearable. The entire Proboscis seemed to vibrate
and shake from the violence of the storm outside.
Claps of thunder echoed Rex's heavy breathing and
pounding heartbeat. The deeper he went into the
massive tube, the stronger the gust pushed up against
him. The increasing wind, combined with the ladder
rushing past, gave him the impression he was falling.

Clump! His feet struck grated metal. His arms and
legs still tingled from the sudden effort, but the tension in his back relaxed now that he could stand up.
He'd landed on a support platform like the one he'd
stopped at earlier. But here there was hardly room to
stand. Nearly twenty Auscultors pressed in together,
all pushing in to get a glimpse of whatever it was that
had been found. Up above, the remaining Auscultors
had to halt on the ladder and hold their positions.
There was no room left on the platform.

"What is it?" Rex asked. He got no answer. As if on cue, all of the Auscultors gathered on the platform spoke at once, their voices creating a disembodied cacophony in Rex's earpiece.

"Oh, my God!"

"How long has it been here?"

"It's just like the others!"

"Can you see outside?"

"I thought the place was empty!"

"What are they doing?"

"What are we going to do?"

"Oh, my God . . . "

Not getting an answer, Rex pushed through the crowd to see what they were looking at. He soon found himself elbowing and even shoving the others aside. But whatever they'd seen had enraptured them so much that they hardly seemed to notice. They seemed stunned—too alarmed to notice anything other than the horrifying spectacle that lay in their midst.

Rex got to the center of the rabble.

There, against the side of Proboscis, a body lay twisted into an unnatural, contorted position. Rex recognized immediately that this was another Cthonian: it was tall, pale, and wearing the same suit he'd seen on the others above. But this one was different.

For one, it wasn't frozen. Given the heat in the Proboscis, that was not surprising. But whereas the ones Rex had seen had been found in a climbing position, this one dangled upside down, suspended aloft by a foot. Rex peered more closely and saw that the body's foot had become lodged in a shredded portion of the Proboscis wall. It looked as if the body had fallen from above, hit the wall here just before the platform, and its foot had gotten caught on one of the massive bolts holding the stratoneum plates together. The force of the fall had caused the body to rip open part of the side of the Proboscis. This had created a gap in the tube's seal big enough for a person to fit through. While the body dangled downward by its foot, the gash created a powerful intake of air that filled the Proboscis with a blast of the outside. The smell the Auscultors had detected had come from the body, which was clearly in full decomposition. Because the hot air had been blowing upward, a sort of vacuum had been created, bathing the Auscultors in the overpowering reek of death.

Ignoring the body, the Auscultors who'd arrived before Rex were stepping up one by one to the gash in the wall to look out. Pulling their faces up close to the hole and fighting against the wind, they peered out, before stepping back and shaking their heads.

Static.

"I can't believe it."

"Did you see how many were down there?"

"What does this mean?"

"What are we going to do?"

"Rex?" Yoné's voice startled Rex, who hadn't realized he'd pushed up next to his Point. He turned to his right and recognized her by her uniform and silhouette.

"You should look out," she said. "I can't believe it."

"The hole?" Rex pointed.

Yoné said nothing. She only nodded.

With nerves taught, Rex stepped up to the gash when a spot opened. He avoided looking too closely at the body, but he saw that it was a girl. From the corner of his eye, he could tell that her skin was just as pale as the others', though by now it had taken a more sickly, yellowish color. Like the others, the Cthonian's mouth and nose were covered by a small face mask. Had she been part of the original team? Had she somehow fallen while the others made it up top? Had she really been down here for more than two days in this heat? That explained the smell . . .

When Rex was within a foot of the gash, he was hit full-force by a gust of wind from outside that caused him to stumble backward. Leaning forward, he shot his arms out and latched them onto the edges of the hole. He pulled. The sound of the rushing wind grew in his ears, quickly drowning out the din of the others' panicked transmissions in his earpiece. He pulled harder, harder, until his head reached the hole and he was able to look out.

The first thing Rex noticed was a dark, dark blue. He must've been staring at the nighttime sky, but then he realized that he was below the Welcans cloud, because the moon was nowhere to be seen and the sky was much darker than he'd ever noticed before. Part of him wanted to look up to get a sense of what the Welcans cloud looked like from underneath, but he knew in the dark he would see nothing.

Rex rotated his head downward. He scanned the horizon and looked toward what he expected to be the ground.

He didn't have to look long before he saw something that horrified him.

There, nearly three miles below his spot on the edge of the Proboscis, Rex saw the angular, organized, glowing form of a network of tents and what looked like a cloth or glass tunnel unfolded across the ground. Rex was clearly looking at some form of settlement—a human settlement. And everything was clumped around the foot of the Proboscis.

Body tingling with fear, Rex scanned the outpost. Through the distance, Rex could make out one main building, like a large tent, that was surrounded by several smaller tents, like annexes. The structures looked temporary, like they could blow over in a strong wind. Apart from the structure, Rex saw no movement—no people, no vehicles, no animals. Just glowing tents.

Static.

"Do you see it?" Yoné's voice crackled. "Rex?"

"Yeah, I see it." Rex's voice wavered as he spoke. He stepped back from the hole to allow someone else to look. He was filled with a blend of awe at seeing something no other Ætherian had ever seen before mixed with the terror of having discovered the origin of whoever those bodies had belonged to. These tents must've been where they'd come from, but there had to be something else—something more significant— that could help them understand why.

"What are they?" Rex asked. His eyes fell on the mangled body. "Has no one ever seen these before? I thought people came down regularly to check the struts and things. What's going on?"

"I don't know. And no, no one's ever seen this before. They came down just a few weeks ago, and there was nothing. So those Cthonians have built all that up just in the past few weeks. But they've also built up those tents right around the Proboscis. And it must be them who's been sending people up."

"Oh, God . . . " Rex's mind drifted to the sight of the bodies lined up in the morgue. Their unnatural tallness. Their massive heads. Their pale skin. And their strange tattoos of an inverted triangle. Something had started and seemed to be underway, but what?

Static.

"We've got to get out of here," Yoné snapped. "Ætheria's not safe anymore."

TEN

BERNUAC HQ WAS IN UPROAR. SIXTY Auscultors, ten Points, Challies, and Roman all seemed to be shouting at each other at once.

By now Rex had turned in his oxygen tank and pulled off his mask, leaving a thin coat of sweat over his face and neck. His whole body was tense, not from the exhaustion of the three-hour descent and nearly five-hour ascent, but from the sheer alarm that filled everyone. People were terrified of who these Cthonians were and what they wanted. People were stunned that there were, in fact, many more Cthonians living below than had been expected.

As people bustled against each other, bumping and pushing to shout to the next nearest person in the crowd, Rex thought once more of the bodies. Their jettisoned message units. Those people—those dead people—had not only maintained some sort of existence for nearly eight hundred years down on Cthonia, but they had just climbed the entire length of the six-mile-high Proboscis . . . just within the past few days. Why? What were they planning? Why had they built those tents so close to the Proboscis? What were they doing? Were they trying to contact the Ætherians? Communicate with them? Why had they not come up until now?

"Auscultors," a calm but booming voice echoed through the room's stentrophones. The roiling heads, arms, and shoulders stilled somewhat, but the bedlam persisted as people talked over each other. Rex recognized the voice as Deputy Head Schlott's. He looked to his right and noticed that Yoné had sidled up to him.

"Let's see what the official take on all this is," she said.

"Any ideas?" Rex asked.

She shook her head. She then nodded toward the front of the room as if to say, "Shh. She's going to tell us."

"Auscultors!" Schlott's voice sounded again. Rex stood on his toes to see over heads and to the front of the room. There, where Challies had spoken to them just hours before, Schlott had planted her feet in the middle of the platform and faced all of them. Her eyes scanned the crowd. Rex noticed that—like Roman and his foster dad—she was still wearing her personal oxygen tank. When they had come back out of the Proboscis, the first thing the Auscultors had to do was submit their own tanks to their Points, who turned them in to the High Command. The tanks then promptly disappeared.

"Auscultors, thank you for listening," Schlott continued. The crowd quieted enough for her to speak at a normal volume, which was still amplified. "We are sure that you have questions about what you have observed. We understand. Believe me, this discovery—this revelation of whatever is going on below, of how these people are accessing the Proboscis—is a shock to us all. But right now," she took a deep breath and scanned the room again. She pulled her shoulders up around her neck as she continued to speak. "Right now you have done your work. The power team at Tátea is still on the island, along with a squadron of armed ACF. They are watching the Proboscis and the functionings on the island closely. So it's business at normal."

Rex knew that meant his foster dad was over on Tátea, working. Had he been working there all night? If so, it wouldn't be the first time.

Schlott's voice brought Rex back to the present and out of his wandering thoughts.

"The leadership within the ACF is, as we speak, analyzing your reports. It is our job to make sense of what has happening. And," she paused, "you all know that as sworn-in recruits to the Ætherian Cover

Force, you are bound to secrecy about what you have seen. About what you have heard. Unit Alif, starting tomorrow your training will shift. You will no longer be Auscultors. Starting tomorrow, we will accelerate your training. You will learn to manage arms in order to defend Ætheria. In the meantime, I and the other members of the ACF leadership will head directly to Tátea to get our preparations underway."

Click. Cli-click. Pop.

The sound of electricity arcing caused Rex and Yoné to jump. Schlott started as well, her eyes darting around the room. She stepped back from the front line of the recruits. Around Rex, other ACF looked around for the source of the sound.

Pop. Pop.

Rex lifted his head to the ceiling as a new sound joined the popping. The soft humming of the fluorescent lights—until then hardly noticeable—flashed on and off, and the tubular light bulbs flickered like a strobe. It was as if someone were jiggling their switch, causing the light to flash.

What was going on?

The crowd looked around: at the walls, the hatch, the ceiling, Schlott . . . The lights flickered once, twice, three times in quick succession.

And then all the power went out. A roar of alarm filled the room. All around Rex, arms and torsos jarred and pressed against him. The feeling was not one of panic, but of agitation. Despite the dark, Rex could feel the tension in the air. Someone's hand reached out and gripped his upper arm. Rex didn't have to ask to know that it was Yoné. She seemed to be trying to keep track of him in the dark.

"Quiet!" Schlott's unamplified voice boomed, filling the room. Rex was surprised at how much power her voice had. The room became still.

"There is no need to get worked up," Schlott continued. "It's just a power outage." Schlott fell silent. Rex thought he heard the general whispering of someone—or several people—but he wasn't sure. As his eyes adjusted to the light, he began to make out the heads and shoulders of those around him. It was just then he realized that the sun must've been coming up outside. Their operation had lasted almost all night and dawn was arriving. It always came early at thirty thousand feet.

Rex leaned over to where he sensed Yoné to be.

"Now what?" he asked.

"Strange," she said. "I've never seen a power outage before. I wonder . . . "

She never finished her sentence.

Outside, someone screamed. And then someone else. Far away, their voices sliced by the piercing wind of the jet stream.

"What's that?!" Rex asked. Others around him must've thought the same thing, because the din in the room quickly grew once more. But this time, Schlott said nothing. In the growing light, Rex tried to squint to where she'd been standing before the power cut. He thought he could just make out several forms in the general area, but he couldn't tell for sure if one of them was hers. Suddenly Yoné's grip on his upper arm became firmer—painful, even.

"Come on!" she hissed, pulling him toward the edge of the room.

"What?!"

"Just come!" Yoné pulled Rex through the crowd and toward the room's exit hatch. Several dozen others were doing the same. ACF recruits poured out of the room and into the transit tubes alongside Bernuac HQ, while others lingered behind. Rex wondered if Schlott was still in the room. Part of him suspected she'd left for some reason. Otherwise, he thought, wouldn't she be shouting for them to all quiet down?

Yoné and Rex made their way outside of the assembly hall and into the transit tube. By now the morning sun was just below the eastern horizon, and the two were bathed in light. Around them, dozens of frightened ACF recruits tramped ahead, their eyes betraying worry. Who had screamed? Where? Rex noticed several of the Points were there as well. A few had drawn their Stær guns. Something was wrong. Something more than just the power outage.

Rex and Yoné reached the transit tube hatch and stepped outside into the glacial, buffeting air whipping around their island. The sixty-mile-per-hour wind ripped and tore at Rex's AG suit, filling his ears with a high, piercing whistle. They were facing south. The other ACF recruits spread out, looking for anything out of the ordinary, and in particular whoever had screamed. Rex scanned the island from the entrance hatch but saw nothing out of the ordinary. Aside from the recruits, there was no one outside. Just the same translucent transit tubes and the same cluster of teardrop-shaped homes lining adjacent islands, which curled around in front of them as the archipelago fanned out. Apart from the wind, nothing was moving.

"Look at that!" one of the Points shouted from off to the right. "Look! It's Tátea!"

Rex shifted his gaze to the right. About a mile away, he could make out Tátea, the bulbous Proboscis reaching over its southernmost edge and stretching downward into the Welcans cloud below.

This was the island he'd seen many times before, but from much closer, as his own home lay on the island directly opposite Ætheria's Power Works. This was the island where Franklin Strapp, his foster father, worked every day of the year to guarantee a steady stream of electricity and water to the stratospheric settlement. It was where his foster father was at that moment.

But when he looked at Tátea now, Rex's breath failed him. With tremendous speed, a continuous ball of fire rocketed up the length of the Proboscis, bursting from the Welcans cloud like an enraged dragon. Something below had ignited the cthoneum gas inside, and Ætheria's energy supply tube was exploding before the Ætherians' eyes. A low rumble filled the air as the flames hurtled upward and lapped at the side of the Power Works where the Proboscis connected to the building. And in the next instant, the building erupted in a massive ball of flame and black smoke that billowed upward in a fifty-yard-wide mushroom cloud. From Rex's spot, the explosion was silent, but two seconds later a gut-wrenching report slammed into the group of ACF standing outside. Some tumbled backwards, some covered their ears, some screamed. As for Rex, his hearing immediately rang deaf from the blast, but he kept his eyes glued in horror on the devastation.

As the ball of flame rose from the island, what was left of the Power Works began to slide toward the edge of Tátea like some giant model about to tumble off of a shelf. Like ants pouring from an overturned anthill, people swarmed out of the power-generating complex, their arms held wide at their sides for balance, and they wobbled and stumbled away from the burning building—toward the closest Zipp line to evacuate. From this far away, Rex could tell by their movements and their darting heads that they were terrified. Some were on fire.

They never made it. As the building reached its mid-point on Tátea's edge, an enormous chunk of the island dislodged and slid away, tumbling into the void. In the crater that remained, what people had escaped fell backwards, sliding down the burnt crater and hurtling below, their arms and legs flailing. Some were able to cling to Tátea's crumbling sides, but soon they lost their grip and fell. Rex tried to see if his foster dad was among them, but couldn't tell at this distance. All he could make out was a smattering of small, dark silhouettes.

Boom! Boomboom!

From somewhere miles below, the dull, muffled thud of explosions slammed into the underside of Bernuac HQ like a massive, invisible wave of air. Rex's feet shook at the tremor.

As if some giant far below had taken the Proboscis and shook it, a shock wave crashed up the length of the stratoneum pipe, dislodging it completely from the side of the smoking crater. Then, as if in slow motion, the millions of tons of reddish stratoneum buckled and folded, crashing below. Geysers of carbon dioxide and water vapor exploded from the mass of tubes, forming a constellation of contrails as the mammoth complex of pipes sank down toward the Welcans cloud. Rex watched in terror as Ætheria's lifeline disappeared soundlessly amid a swish of yellow vapor. Some of the people gathered along the pathway screamed; others wept. Moments later, a muffled roar of thunder roiled up from Cthonia.

The remains of the Power Works and the Proboscis now lay in a heap of destruction six miles below.

As the Power Works and Proboscis disappeared amid flame and smoke, spots danced before Rex's eyes as reality tried to pry its way into his consciousness.

He fell to his knees and crawled toward the edge of the island, trying to spot any remains of the structure that kept them all alive. But all he saw was the same, roiling yellow clouds he'd seen all his life. Around him, people ran about. People clutched each other for support. People cried. People cursed. People collapsed.

"Dad!" he screamed. "Dad!" And then, almost inexplicably, "Mom!"

Rex gasped for breath in the face of the tragedy.

But it was no use.

His entire family was gone.